# THE
# PERFECT
# GENTLEMAN

## Also by Marion Chesney in Large Print:

Belinda Goes to Bath
Colonel Sandhurst to the Rescue
Daphne
Deborah Goes to Dover
The Deception
The Intrigue
Lady Fortescue Steps Out
French Affair
Emily Goes to Exeter
Back in Society
The Banishment
The First Rebellion
The Sins of Lady Dacey
Enlightening Delilah

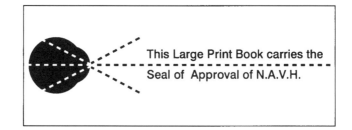

This Large Print Book carries the
Seal of Approval of N.A.V.H.

# THE
# PERFECT
# GENTLEMAN

## Marion Chesney

**G.K. Hall & Co.**
**Thorndike, Maine**

Copyright © 1988 by Marion Chesney

Published in 1997 by arrangement with Ballantine/Fawcett Books, a division of Random House, Inc.

G.K. Hall Large Print Romance Collection.

The text of this Large Print edition is unabridged. Other aspects of the book may vary from the original edition.

Set in 16 pt. Plantin.

Printed in the United States on permanent paper.

**Library of Congress Cataloging in Publication Data**

Chesney, Marion.
    The perfect gentleman : the paper princess / Marion Chesney.
      p.  cm.
    ISBN 0-7838-8257-2 (lg. print : hc : alk. paper)
    1. Large type books.   I. Title.
  [PR6053.H4535P46  1997]
  823´.914—dc21                         97-17829

9\15

# THE PERFECT GENTLEMAN

# Chapter One

The marriage proposal of Lord Andrew Childe, younger son of the Duke and Duchess of Parkworth, was everything it should have been.

For Lord Andrew did everything well. He was handsome and faultlessly dressed. He was a famous whip, he boxed with Gentleman Jackson, he read ancient Greek easily, and he wrote witty poems in Latin.

He saw no reason to trouble himself by pursuing some debutante at the London Season. Some time before it had begun, before the leaves were yet on the trees, he had singled out Miss Ann Worthy as his future bride.

Lord Andrew was thirty-two and considered young misses insipid. Miss Worthy was twenty-eight and hailed from the untitled aristocracy. From her long, aristocratic nose to her long, narrow feet, she was every inch a lady. She never betrayed any vulgar excess of emotion or committed any common faux pas.

Only an admirer of Lord Byron or some such woolly headed creature would have criticized Lord Andrew's proposal, might have pointed out that the very passionless chilliness of it showed a sad flaw in the character of the Perfect Gentleman — Lord Andrew's nickname.

He had broached the matter to her parents first

and had been accepted by them.

He was left alone with Miss Worthy for a short space of time in the blue saloon of the Worthys' town house in Curzon Street.

Miss Worthy was sitting in front of a tambour frame, neatly putting stitches into a design of bluebells. She affected not to know what was in the air.

He stood in the doorway for a moment, watching her.

She was attired in an expensive morning gown of tucked and ruched white muslin. A cap of pleated muslin almost hid the thick tresses of her red hair. Her nose was long and straight, and her mouth small enough to please the highest stickler. Her pale green eyes veiled by red and gold lashes might have been thought to be a trifle too close-set. Her hands were very long and white.

Although she knew very well Lord Andrew was standing there, and why he had come, she continued to stitch for that short minute before turning her head and affecting a start of surprise.

"Lord Andrew!" she exclaimed. She rose with a graceful movement and went to sit on a backless sofa in front of the cold fireplace — for the Worthys did not light fires after the first of March, no matter what the weather.

"Good afternoon, Miss Worthy," said Lord Andrew. "I trust I find you well?"

"Very well, my lord. Pray be seated."

He was carrying his hat, cane, and gloves — that traditional sign that a gentleman did not intend to stay very long. He laid them down on a small table, approached the sofa, and fell to one knee in front of her.

"Miss Worthy," he said, "I have leave from your parents to pay my addresses to you. I wish to marry you. Will you accept me?"

"Yes, my lord."

He stood up and took her hand and drew her to her feet. He bent his head and kissed her on the mouth. The day was cold. Icy lips met icy lips in a chaste embrace.

Right on cue, Mr. and Mrs. Worthy made their entrance. The happy couple stood hand in hand, gracefully accepting congratulations. Mr. Worthy, thin and ascetic and longing to get back to his beloved books, called for champagne after having been nudged in the ribs by his small, dumpy wife.

Lord Andrew took a glass, toasted his fiancée, toasted his future in-laws, and then took his leave.

All just as it should have been.

With the long, easy stride of a practiced athlete, he walked to his parents' house in Park Lane — although it, like the neighboring houses, still faced onto Park Street. Not so long ago Park Lane had been Tyburn Lane of dubious repute. There was not much of a view of Hyde Park, for the high wall which had been built to screen the residents from the condemned on their way to the scaffold was still there. One enterprising resident had had part of the wall removed and the entrance to his house made leading from Park Lane itself, but the rest still preferred to keep to Park Street, which was still the front entrance for the rest of the houses.

Up until that moment when he walked into his parents' house and made his way to the library, Lord Andrew would have considered himself the most fortunate and happiest of men. Unlike most younger sons, he was very rich, having been given one of the minor ducal houses and estates as his own. By studying all the latest innovations in scientific farming, he had made it prosper. The money from his estates had been carefully invested. He could have afforded his own town house and could have lived completely independently from his family if he chose.

But the Duchess of Parkworth had managed to turn the large town house into a home. It had an air of ease and prettiness and elegance. Lord Andrew found it restful.

In his early years, he had not seen very much of his parents from one year's end to the other. He had an excellent tutor whose job it was to turn him into a gentleman. Lord Andrew had admired this tutor greatly. And so Lord Andrew went to Oxford University, and then on the Grand Tour with his tutor, and then into the army to "round him off."

When his tutor, Mr. Blackwell, died while he was away at the wars, Lord Andrew felt as if he had lost a father. Mr. Blackwell had orchestrated the forming of Lord Andrew's character, down to choosing his tailor. He had even seen to it that my lord had lost his virginity at a suitably early age at the hands of a lusty and bawdy housemaid. That last experience had caused Lord Andrew to acquire a certain distaste for the female sex. But on the whole, he was happy and carefree and interested in perfecting everything he turned his hand to, always trying to live up to the high standards of his now deceased tutor.

But as he sat down in the library and gazed at the flickering flames of the fire, he felt, for the first time, uncomfortable inside his own skin.

Usually when he had done just as he ought, he could see in his mind's eye Mr. Blackwell's smile of approval. But all he could think of was that chilly kiss. What else did he expect? Marriage was one thing, lust another.

He usually looked forward to the Season as a break from the cares of agriculture. He enjoyed racing and fencing and dancing, the opera, plays, and parties. He did not have to attend the House of Lords. That chore fell to the eldest son, the Marquess of Bridgeworth, who enjoyed making long and boring speeches on the game laws.

But for the first time, Lord Andrew began to feel uneasily bored. He remembered when he had been very small, his nurse promising to take him to the servants' Christmas party. He had lain awake for nights before the great event, trembling with anticipation. But then his nurse had told him that his mother, the duchess, had learned of her plans, and he was not to attend.

He had not cried, for he knew even then that men of five years old did not cry. But life had seemed to lose color for quite a long time afterwards.

That was what he felt like now, as if he had just experienced a disappointment.

He shook himself and decided his spleen must be disordered from lack of exercise. He would go riding in the park.

He was just about to leave the library and go to his room and change into his riding dress when his father came in.

The duke was small, burly, and undistinguished. He was wearing a banyan wrapped round his thick body and a turban on his head. The banyan was of peacock silk and the oriental turban was of cloth-of-gold, but he still looked more like a bad-tempered farmer than a duke.

"How do?" he grunted. "See the *Gentleman's Magazine* anywhere?"

"Yes, over on the table."

"Good, good," said the duke, shuffling forward to pick it up.

"I proposed to Miss Worthy, Father, and she accepted."

"Well, of course she would," said the duke, picking up the magazine and fishing in his bosom for his quizzing glass.

Lord Andrew smiled. "You think me a great catch, then?"

"Oh, no," said the duke, riffling through the pages. "The Worthys have been hanging out for a title this age. She's got a good dowry, Miss Worthy, and she could have married Mr. Benjamin Jepps this age, but they'd all set their hearts on a title."

"You did not tell me that," said Lord Andrew stiffly.

"Didn't I? Didn't seem important. She's good family, and you ain't exactly in the first blush of youth."

"Yet I am not in my dotage."

"Grrmph," said his father, settling himself down in a wing chair and studying an article in the magazine.

"When does Mother come to town?"

"Hey, what's that?"

"I asked when Mother was coming to town," said Lord Andrew patiently.

"Next week," said the duke, "with this Miss Whatsit she's bringing out."

"Mother sponsoring another debutante? Why was I not told of this?"

"Why should you be? Not your home. Got enough blunt of your own to buy your own house. Why don't you?"

"I would have thought my dear mother and father would have been glad of my company," said Lord Andrew acidly.

"That's common!" said the duke, much shocked. "You've been seeing too many plays. You'll be sitting on my knee next."

"Hardly," said the six-foot-tall Sir Andrew caustically. "Anyway, who is Miss Whatsit, and why is Mama bringing her out?"

"I don't know," said the duke tetchily. "Some parish waif. You know what your mother's like. Lame ducks underfoot the whole time. Poor relations, plain Janes who can't get a husband. Whoever this Miss Whatsit is, you can take it from me she'll be as ugly as sin and won't own a penny. Your mother will have her all puffed up with consequence and vanity, she won't take, and she'll be sent back to the country with a lot of useless airs and graces and marry the curate. Now, run along, do," he added, as if Lord Andrew were still in shortcoats.

Lord Andrew went off to exercise the blue devils out of his system. He rode hard that day, he fenced, he boxed, and then, feeling tired and slightly better, he made his way home again. But as he walked past a row of shops in South Molton Street just as the light was fading, he saw an interesting tableau in the upstairs window of an apartment above a butcher's shop.

The little shopkeeper's parlor was ablaze with candles. The butcher and his wife, dressed in their best, were facing a young couple, a pretty girl and a tall, honest-looking young man. The young man said something and took the girl's hand in his. The girl blushed and lowered her eyes. The young man put his hand on his heart. The butcher's wife began to cry happy tears, and the butcher raised his burly arms in a blessing.

Lord Andrew felt a queer little tug at his heart. Had he not been the son of a duke, had he been, say, the son of a shopkeeper, he would have been brought up close to his parents. His engagement would have been a celebration, thanks would have been given to God, and he would have received his father's blessing.

A cold wind blew an old newspaper against his legs, and he angrily kicked it away.

Among their many properties, the Duke and Duchess of Parkworth owned the Sussex village of Lower Bexham. The squire, Sir Hector Mortimer, had recently died, leaving a pile of debt to his one surviving child, Penelope.

The vicar of St. Magnus the Martyr, the church in Lower Bexham, had written to the duchess about young Penelope's plight.

The duchess wrote back immediately, promising to call on this Miss Mortimer. The Duchess of Parkworth had a soft heart, easily touched, but unfortunately, although she started off with enthusiasm to help her lame ducks, she could not sustain any interest in them for long. She was lame duckless for the moment. The previous charge had been a young footman who had confessed to a longing to be an army captain. The duchess had arranged everything and then had promptly forgotten about the footman. Even when she got a sad little letter from the footman saying he would have to resign his commission, for without any private income, he could not pay his mess bills, she had pettishly thrown it away, saying, "It is of no use to go on helping people who cannot help themselves."

Fortunately for him, the footman had the wit to then write to Lord Andrew, who investigated his capabilities as a soldier, sorted out his debts, and arranged an allowance for him. When the duchess learned that the ex-footman was still a captain, and when she had not heard further from him, she had gone about saying, "There you are! People must stand on their own two feet."

She descended on Penelope Mortimer suffused with all the warm glow of a Lady Bountiful.

Penelope Mortimer's appearance came as rather a shock. The duchess was used to forwarding the careers of plain girls. Penelope had blond, almost silver hair, with a natural curl. Her blue eyes were wide and well spaced and fringed with sooty lashes. Her figure was dainty. She was a trifle small in stature.

Miss Mortimer's one remaining servant introduced the duchess, who sailed in like a galleon. The duchess was almost as tall as Lord Andrew, but a liking for food had given her a massive figure, which she tried to reduce by wearing sturdy whalebone corsets. She had a small head and small hands and feet. Her massive figure did not seem to belong to her. It was as if she had poked her head through the cardboard cutout of a fat lady at the fairground.

The duchess was enchanted by Penelope's appearance and manner. She had not been in the house for ten minutes before she was already weaving dreams about what a sensation Penelope would be at the Season.

Penelope, bewildered by plans for her social debut, tried to explain where matters stood. Her mother had died some years previously, her father the year before. Penelope had sold up everything that could be sold, and most of the debts had been paid. She had put her home on the market and had already selected a comfortable little cottage in the village. She had not once considered coming out. In order to explain to this overwhelming duchess about the exact state of her financial straits, Penelope excused herself and then returned with a pile of accounts' ledgers, all written out in her neat hand. She popped a pair of steel spectacles on her nose and began to explain the figures to the duchess.

But the duchess was staring in horror at those spectacles. Penelope's dreaming expression had disappeared the minute she put those spectacles on, and her eyes gleamed with a most unbecomingly sharp intelligence.

"No, no, no!" said her grace, snatching the spectacles from Penelope's little nose. "You must never wear these dreadful things again!"

"But I must, Your Grace," said Penelope. "I am quite blind without them. How will I be able to read?"

"Books!" said the duchess with loathing. "Young ladies are better off without them, and although I am sure your accounts are correct, it is most unladylike of you to be able to do such things."

"Through lack of money," said Penelope firmly, "I am become used to doing quite a lot of things that young ladies are not supposed to do. I garden and I cook. I find useful occupation most entertaining."

"Horrors!" said the duchess, raising her little hands in the air.

"In fact, Your Grace, you must not concern yourself with my future. Once I sell this house, I shall have enough to live on for quite some time. I have already put up a sign as a music teacher and have five pupils."

The duchess's mouth sagged in a disappointed droop. This gorgeous creature simply must come to London.

She pulled herself up to her full height. "You have no choice in the matter, Miss Mortimer. I command you to pack your things and come with me!"

There was nothing else Penelope could do. The duke and duchess owned the village. Ever practical, Penelope complied. She would try to enjoy herself at the Season and then return to the village.

A week later, she set out for London, a week during which she had asked and asked for her spectacles only to be told that the duchess "had them safe" but that they were too unbecoming. She presented Penelope with a tiny gold quizzing glass and told her to make the best of that.

At first Penelope tried to accept the loss of her spectacles philosophically. She knew that ladies did not wear them in public and that officers' wives were actually forbidden to wear them. The poor Duchess of Wellington dreaded going out in her carriage, for she was very shortsighted and could not recognize anyone, but even she had to abide by the social laws and leave her spectacles at home. But on the road to London, Penelope began to think of ways to get them back, hoping the duchess had kept them by her. To this end, she passed most of the journey making friends with the duchess's lady's maid, Perkins, and finally discovering that Perkins herself had the spectacles in safekeeping.

By the time the carriage rolled along Park Street, Penelope had those spectacles back in her own reticule after many promises to Perkins that she would never let the duchess know she had them.

Their arrival was late at night, and so Penelope did not see any of the other occupants of the house. She drank a glass of hot wine and water given to her by Perkins, popped her glasses on her nose, fished a novel out of her luggage, and began to read, putting all this nonsense about the Season firmly out of her mind. On the journey to London, Penelope had become even firmer in her resolve to endure it all as best she could and then return to freedom.

She awoke early despite the fact she had been reading a good part of the night. The bedroom that had been assigned to her was much grander than any room Penelope had slept in before. The bed was luxuriously soft and had a canopy of white lace. There was white lace everywhere — bed hangings, curtains, laundry bag, and even the doilies on the toilet table.

Feeling rather gritty and dirty, Penelope rang the bell and shyly asked the chambermaid who answered it if she might have a bath. But no, that was not possible, was the reply. Water was pumped to the London houses three days a week, and today was not a water day.

Penelope stripped off and did the best she could with the cans of water on the toilet table.

She put on a pretty white muslin with a blue spot and then ventured downstairs. The great house was hushed and quiet. Penelope knew from reading the social news in the papers that the great of London often did not rise until two in the afternoon. But she was very hungry.

A footman was crossing the hall as she came down the stairs, and to her request, he replied that it would be served in the morning room as Lord Andrew liked an early breakfast.

The morning room, he said, was on the first floor on the left. Penelope retreated up the stairs and pushed open the door.

A pleasant smell of coffee and hot toast greeted her. There was a tall man already seated at a table by the window. Penelope could not see him very clearly, but she gained an impression he was black-haired and handsome.

He rose to his feet at her entrance, bowed, and pulled out a chair for her. "You must be Miss

Mortimer," he said in a pleasant voice. "I am Childe."

Penelope blinked and then stifled a giggle. It was rather like meeting one of those savages portrayed in the romances she liked to read where a savage would say to the bewildered heroine stranded on some foreign shore, "Me man." Then she remembered Lord Andrew Childe was the duchess's younger son.

"What is amusing you?" asked Lord Andrew.

"It was a nervous giggle," said Penelope primly. "This is a ducal mansion. I am not used to such grandeur. It unnerves me."

"Indeed!" Lord Andrew thought little Miss Mortimer looked very composed. She was not his mama's usual choice of protégée, for there was no denying that Miss Mortimer was remarkably pretty. But there was a vacant, unseeing look in those beautiful eyes of hers which marked a lack of intelligence, thought Lord Andrew. Therefore, after he had helped her to toast and coffee, he was not at all surprised when Penelope asked him, "Do you read novels, Lord Andrew?"

"No," he said with the kind of indulgent smile he reserved for the weaker-brained. "I consider them a great waste of time."

"Life would be very boring without imagination and romance," said Penelope. "Reality can be fatiguing."

"Nonsense. Retreating into novels shows a sad lack of courage. What do you find in the real world so distressing, Miss Mortimer?"

Penelope held up one little hand, rough and reddened from her gardening and cooking, and ticked off the items on her fingers. "My father died last year. One. He left a monstrous pile of debt. Two. I thought I had solved my future and my financial problems when the Duchess of Parkworth arrived and told me I must have a Season. Three," she ended with a final flick of the third finger.

"I see. I am sorry to hear of your father's death and of your troubles. I agree with the first two items, but surely a Season is to be enjoyed!"

"But I didn't want a Season," said Penelope reasonably. "I wanted to be left alone."

"Then you have only to tell my mother that," he said stiffly.

"Oh, but I did!" said Penelope. "And she commanded me to come with her, and as your family owns our village, I could not very well refuse."

"Of course you could have refused. This is not the Middle Ages. Did you expect my mama to take some sort of revenge had you not complied with her wishes?"

"Something like that."

"Now, there we have a good example of the pernicious effect of novels," said Lord Andrew. "You have been imagining all sorts of Gothic nonsense."

"I have?" Penelope tried to bring his face into focus, but it remained a vaguely handsome blur. She had been warned that screwing up your eyes gave you premature wrinkles, and although she was not vain, she had no desire to look old before her time. So to Lord Andrew, her expression appeared vacant and rather stupid.

"Do not trouble yourself further," he said. "I shall speak to my mother today. You will find yourself returned to the country as quickly as possible."

"Thank you," said this irritating beauty meekly. "But you will find it will not serve."

# Chapter Two

Knowing his mother would sleep late, Lord Andrew walked round to the Worthys' home in Cavendish Square. Miss Ann Worthy had often assured him she was up with the lark.

But although it was nearly ten in the morning, he was told that the whole family was still in bed. Unable to believe his love could be other than truthful, he commanded the butler to take up a message requesting Miss Worthy to come riding with him that afternoon at two.

Ann Worthy was not amused at being awoken at dawn, as she put it. She was further annoyed by Lord Andrew's invitation. She and her parents were to go that afternoon to visit relatives in Primrose Hill. The relatives included four unmarried misses in their teens. Ann was looking forward to putting their noses out of joint with the announcement of her engagement.

Besides, what was the point of going driving at two in the afternoon? Five was the fashionable hour. There was no one in London at two, thought Miss Worthy, carelessly dismissing the other ninety-eight percent of the town's population from her mind.

She was to see Lord Andrew at the opera that evening. It would do him no harm to learn early that she was not prepared to be at his beck and call. With a novel feeling of power, Miss Worthy sent back a note with the intelligence that she was not free that afternoon. She did not trouble to give any explanation.

Lord Andrew found himself becoming highly irritated. He did not believe Miss Worthy was in bed, for surely since she was not given to extravagances of speech and would not make claims to be an early riser were it not true, he felt she might at least have had the courtesy to receive him.

He did not know that a great deal of his irritation sprang from an unrealized desire to see her again as soon as possible to allay that nagging doubt at the back of his mind.

That he had any doubts about his engagement, he would not admit to himself. Miss Worthy was of good family, she was a lady, and he had made a careful choice. He had done the right thing — as usual — but unusually, doing the right thing had not brought its usual mild glow of satisfaction.

He went for a solitary ride in the park, where he remembered the plight of Miss Mortimer. He smiled indulgently as he recalled the silly little thing's fears about his mother taking revenge.

He rode home and strode up to the morning room. His mother was reading a newspaper, squinting horribly at the print.

"You need spectacles, Mama," he said.

"Nonsense! The light is bad here. Those trees quite take away the sun."

Lord Andrew glanced about the bright room, at the sunlight sparkling on the silver of the coffeepot, but decided argument would be useless.

"Put down that paper, Mama," he said. "I wish to talk about Miss Mortimer."

"Penelope," said the duchess with a fond smile. "Such a dear little thing, and so exquisitely pretty. I declare she will turn all heads."

"But it appears that Miss Mortimer does not wish a Season. She assures me she would be perfectly happy to return to the country. Although she is lacking in intelligence, she does appear to have a certain decided opinion of what she does want. I pointed out to her that she had only to tell you, and you would be happy to let her go."

The duchess's face took on a rather sulky look. "Fiddle. Girls of that age do not know their own minds. And what, pray, is a more pleasant way of occupying a girl's mind than parties and balls?"

"I assure you, that is not the case with Miss Mortimer."

"I know what is best for her," said the duchess. "She must be guided by me. Just wait until Maria Blenkinsop sees my charge! She is bringing out a plain little antidote who she has the gall to say will take the town by storm. When she sees my Penelope, she will change her tune."

"You leave me no alternative," said Lord Andrew. "It appears I must make arrangements myself to send Miss Mortimer back to the country."

The duchess's pale gray eyes hardened. "You

may have forgot, my dear boy, that we own that village in which she resides. She has to sell her father, the squire's, house, and plans to buy that little cottage at the end of Glebe Street near the parsonage ground. She has hopes of securing a lease. But I am sure there are others who would be equally interested in that cottage. Quite a sound building, and in good repair."

Her son looked at her in horror. "Are you saying you would punish Miss Mortimer were she to return?"

"No, I did not say that," lied his mother. "What is all this to you, Andrew? You are engaged to exactly the sort of female I would expect you to propose to. . . ."

"Meaning?"

"Never mind. But this is not your house, and Miss Mortimer has nothing to do with you. Why do you not go about your own business and stop meddling in mine? I am sure your fiancée will be desirous of a visit from you."

"Miss Worthy is engaged elsewhere this afternoon."

"Splendid!" said the duchess. "You shall take Miss Mortimer on a drive. She cannot appear anywhere tonish until I have ordered her wardrobe."

"I shall do no such thing."

Lord Andrew had never crossed swords with his mother before. He had dealt with the matter of the footman-turned-captain without telling her about it. He had never before realized that her passion for her lame ducks was so very strong. He was horrified to see tears start to the duchess's eyes. Her whole massive body shook with sobs, and her small face above it pouted like a pug's.

"You never cared for me," hiccuped the duchess. "Never. You always were an unnatural and unfeeling boy. Oh! When I am on my deathbed, then you will wish you had tried to please me. Angels come and take me! My son spurns me. Ah, what is left?"

"I'll take the brat out," shouted Lord Andrew. "Where is she?"

"In the drawing room," said the duchess from behind the cover of her handkerchief.

Lord Andrew stormed out.

The morning room had two doors, one leading from the landing and another from the backstairs. The duke entered by the one from the backstairs, holding a cup of chocolate in one hand and a pile of letters in the other.

"What was all that screaming about?" he asked.

"Nothing, my dear," said the duchess placidly. "I was just having a little talk to Andrew."

Penelope looked up in surprise as the door of the drawing room crashed open. She had only a bare second in which to whip off her spectacles before Lord Andrew, still in his riding dress, marched into the room.

"You are coming driving with me," he said abruptly. "Get your bonnet."

"There is no need to shout," said Miss

Penelope Mortimer primly. "I did warn you she would not be moved on the matter."

"What are you talking about?" roared Lord Andrew.

"I'll get my bonnet," said Penelope, scrambling from the room.

Lord Andrew looked down at his riding dress. He wondered whether to change and then reflected he could not be bothered going to the effort to please such as Miss Mortimer.

That was the first crack in his perfection, for Lord Andrew had hitherto always worn the correct dress for the occasion.

Penelope selected a gypsy straw bonnet embellished on the crown with marguerites, and tied it firmly under her chin by its gold silk ribbons. She put on her one, good pelisse, her last present from her father. It was of gold-embroidered silk and lined with fur. She had a longing to see what Lord Andrew really looked like, and so when she returned to the drawing room, she opened the door very quietly, raised her quizzing glass which was hanging round her neck, and studied him as he stood by the window looking out over the park.

Lord Andrew sprang into focus. He had thick, glossy black hair cut in the Windswept. He had a high-profiled, handsome face and a firm, uncompromising mouth. His black riding coat was tailored by the hand of a master. His white cravat was intricately pleated and folded. He was wearing breeches and top boots.

She dropped the glass quickly before he turned around, and was idiotically glad he had changed back into a comfortable blur instead of the disturbingly arrogant and handsome man she had seen through the quizzing glass.

"I am driving an open carriage," he said. "It is being brought round from the mews. It is quite correct for you to go out with me without a chaperone."

"I am glad you are at liberty, sir," said Penelope. "I would have thought your time would have been occupied in squiring Miss Worthy."

"Has my mother told you already of my engagement?"

"I did not know you were engaged," said Penelope. "Her Grace remarked on the journey to London that you were courting a Miss Ann Worthy and would no doubt propose to her. May I offer my congratulations?"

"Thank you." He walked across the room and held open the door. They went down the stairs together and out into Park Street.

He helped her into a smart phaeton, seated himself beside her, and nodded to the groom to stand away from the horses' heads.

Soon they were bowling through the park. It was a sunny, brisk day, and the young leaves were just coming out on the trees. Penelope could see things at a distance quite well, and so she settled back to enjoy the prospect. It was only when she realized they were going round the ring for the second time that she ventured to say shyly, "I do not know London at all well. Would it inconvenience you too much to take me somewhere else?"

"Where would you like to go?"

"I would like to see the wild beasts at the Tower."

He was about to refuse, for he could not think of a more vulgar or tedious way of passing the afternoon, but his tutor had always instructed him to be gallant to the ladies. She was his mother's guest, and her wishes must come first.

"Then we shall go to the Tower," he said in a colorless voice.

He began to be amused as they drove along Oxford Street by Penelope's exclamations of delight at the goods in the shop windows. As the shop windows were just about the right distance from the carriage for her to make out things with her faulty vision, Penelope hung on to the side of the phaeton and watched everything and everyone.

"I wonder if the duchess will let me actually shop for a few things," she said wistfully. "I am a good needle-woman, and it is so much more economical, you know, to make one's own things. I have become used to being busy."

"You must ask her, for I cannot be the judge of what goes on in my mother's mind," he said stiffly.

"So she *did* say she would be displeased if I left — to the point of making life awkward for me?" said Penelope.

"That, too, you must find out for yourself."

"You do not appear to be well acquainted with your mother," remarked Penelope.

There was a trace of amusement in her voice, and he looked at her sharply, but her face under the pretty bonnet was demure.

"No, not very well," he agreed after a pause. "Naturally, I spent my youth with first my nurse and then my tutor. When I grew up, I was away a great deal. My father gave me Baxley Manor and estates in Shropshire, and it is there I made my home. This will be my second Season in London since returning from the wars. My parents are somewhat strangers to me."

"But even in a great household, the children are brought down in the evenings to join the family; is it not so?"

"Not always. Not in my case. Do not look so sad, Miss Mortimer; I had every comfort and a good upbringing. It is those novels you read which lead you to sentimental thoughts of a mother's love."

"It is mine own inclination, sir," said Penelope tartly, "which leads me to ideas of motherly love. I am convinced I should be quite a doting mother. But as I am not likely to put it to the test, I shall be unable to offer you any proof."

"Miss Mortimer, with your face and figure, not to mention my mother's patronage, you will be married before the end of the Season."

"Not I," she said calmly. "My mind is quite

made up. Her Grace wishes to produce me at the Season because she considers my looks of a high order. She wishes to compete with her friends."

"You are too harsh," said Lord Andrew. "You are not the first young miss my parent has sponsored. Certainly the prettiest, but by no means the first. She enjoys helping people in trouble."

"Highly commendable. Did Her Grace have a protégé last Season?"

"Yes."

"Tell me about her. Was she a success? Did she marry and live happily ever after?"

Again he looked at her sharply, for there had been, he was sure, a definite hint of mockery in her voice, but she turned her beautiful vague eyes to his and gave him a sweet smile.

"No," he said. "She was a Miss Thornton, a cousin of mine four times removed. Very little dowry and previously accustomed to a modest style of life. She was plain and rather silly. She did not 'take.' "

"Oh, poor Miss Thornton."

"I would not pity her. She had a great many airs and graces before the Season was over and bullied the Park Street servants quite dreadfully. Mother sent her packing."

"At the end of the Season?"

"No, before then. I do not wish to discuss the matter any further."

Lord Andrew remembered the obnoxious Miss Thornton, whose silly head had been quite turned by the duchess's favors. She was allowed

33

to do as she pleased, to eat chocolates and read novels most of the day, and to go to balls and parties for most of the night. But the unlovely creature had been an object of pity on the day the duchess became tired of her. He wondered how long it would be before his mother tired of Miss Mortimer.

It took longer to get to the Tower of London than he had expected, for no sooner had Miss Mortimer seen the bulk of St. Paul's than she demanded to be taken inside. He himself had privately long considered the famous cathedral a depressing barn of a place, but Miss Mortimer dutifully went over it all.

When they left, he suggested they should return home and see the Tower on another day, but Penelope apologized so prettily for having wasted so much time and said that the Tower was so very close that he finally capitulated.

The menagerie was as smelly and depressing as he remembered it to be. He walked away a little and left Penelope to examine the cages.

The cages were not very big, and so Penelope could only dimly make out the animal shapes inside. She was wildly disappointed. She had left her spectacles at home, but even if she had brought them, the stern social laws would have prevented her from putting them on. Then she remembered the quizzing glass the duchess had given her. She put it to one eye, and a lion sprang into view.

A careless keeper who had just fed the animals

had left the door of the lion's cage open. Penelope walked closer and closer, assuming that the closeness of the animal was due to the strong magnification of the glass.

The lion opened its cavernous mouth and let out a warning rumble. But Penelope, with one eye screwed shut and the glass at the other, did not realize she had walked into the cage, and thought herself still on the safe side of the bars.

And that was the interesting scene which met Lord Andrew's horrified gaze when he turned around.

There was dainty little Miss Mortimer standing over a large lion, holding a quizzing glass, and calmly looking down its throat.

The day had become hazy and golden. The little tableau looked unreal. But he hesitated only a moment.

He was frightened to make a sudden movement for fear of startling the animal, and frightened to call for the keeper, knowing the resultant shouts and screams might make the lion spring.

He walked slowly into the cage, inching toward Penelope.

"Miss Mortimer," he said in a quiet voice, "do not move suddenly or scream, no matter what happens."

The lion gave a full-throated roar. Penelope dropped her quizzing glass in fright and realized the lion was right at her feet, for that animal blur of hair and teeth must be the lion.

Lord Andrew put a strong arm around her

waist, lifted her up in his arms, and began to back away. The lion, made sleepy by food, began to follow them slowly.

"Good God," muttered Lord Andrew. "The beast is going to follow us across London."

A startled cry from the keeper at the other end of the row of cages nearly made him drop Penelope. He darted backwards to safety and slammed the door of the cage shut.

"What were you doin' of?" demanded the red-faced keeper, coming up to them. "Them hanimals ain't for playin' with. You Peep-o-Day boys is all the same."

"It is your own cursed carelessness in leaving the cage door open which has brought about this folly," said Lord Andrew.

He turned and marched away with Penelope still in his arms.

"You can put me down now," said Penelope.

He set her on her feet and glared down at her. "How could you be so stupid?" he raged. "What possessed you? Why walk straight into the lion's cage?"

It somehow did not dawn on him that Penelope was longsighted. Practically every member of the ton carried a quizzing glass. The use of it was an art in itself. Many of them were made of plain glass.

Penelope opened her mouth to confess to her longsightedness. But her mother and father had considered it a terrible defect in a lady and had trained her to conceal it on all occasions and never to be seen with spectacles on. She had not troubled to keep up their standards after her father died, but all the stories she had heard of gentlemen taking an acute dislike to longsighted ladies came back into her mind. Normally sensible, Penelope was made silly by a sudden desire not to appear ugly in Lord Andrew's eyes.

"I am sorry," she said, hanging her head. "I have never seen a lion before, and I was so fascinated, I just kept walking closer and closer."

"If you ladies would stop playing around with those silly quizzing glasses, you might see where you are going," said Lord Andrew, glaring at the top of her bent head.

"I *have* apologized," said Penelope huffily. "The least you can do is accept the apology."

"Very well," he said. "Now may I take you home before you get up to any more mischief?"

Penelope tried to start up a conversation on the road back, but Lord Andrew only replied in monosyllables, and at last she fell silent. Lord Andrew was rapidly coming to the conclusion that Miss Mortimer was a trifle simple. He wondered whether she was a result of inbreeding. The fright he had received on seeing her peering down the lion's throat was still with him, and he blamed her bitterly for that fright.

When they arrived in Park Street, he made Penelope a stiff bow and went in search of his mother. She was in the drawing room, studying fashion plates and swatches of cloth.

"Oh, Andrew, you are back," said the duchess amiably. "Tell me what you think of this pink muslin for Miss Mortimer. White is so insipid."

"Mama," he said patiently, "do not concern yourself further with choosing a wardrobe for Miss Mortimer. She is leaving." He crisply outlined the events of the afternoon. The duchess had deliberately put Penelope's longsightedness out of her mind. There should be no flaw in her latest interest.

"I am sure you exaggerate," she said mildly, and fell to studying the pages of the fashion magazine on her lap.

He took the magazine away from her and sat down opposite. "You must be guided by me," he said seriously. "I agree that Miss Mortimer is vastly pretty. But she is not of our rank. She is only the daughter of a country squire and cannot hope to marry above her station. She is alarmingly lacking in wit."

The duchess's well-corseted bosom swelled dangerously. "She is *not going anywhere*," she said harshly. "Go away, and do not trouble me on this matter again."

"Mama . . ."

"You don't love me," cried the duchess. "You never have! You never have had the least spark of feeling. You do not stay here out of any filial warmth but because it suits your pocket not to have an establishment of your own. Ah, your indifference strikes sharp knives into my maternal bosom!"

Lord Andrew turned red. "There has never been any closeness between us," he said. "I barely know my parents, and it is not of my doing."

The duchess held a vinaigrette to her nose and took a noisy sniff at its contents.

"It was all your own doing, not mine, Andrew. All your love was for that tutor of yours, Blackwell."

"May I point out that when Mr. Blackwell wrote to you from Oxford University and suggested I spend a year at home before going on the Grand Tour, you wrote in reply you could not be troubled."

"That's right, it's all *my* fault!" screamed the duchess. "You unnatural and unfeeling child. Oh, my heart." She slapped her hand somewhere in the region of her heart, and her corsets let out a creak of protest. She swayed in her chair. "Water," she whispered.

Thoroughly alarmed, Lord Andrew rang the bell, and when Perkins, the maid, promptly answered it, he told her to see to her mistress.

"Tell him to go away," moaned the duchess faintly. Perkins looked helplessly at Lord Andrew, who hesitated only a moment before leaving the room.

When the door closed behind him, the duchess straightened up and said briskly, "Do not fuss, Perkins. Go and fetch Miss Mortimer. I wish to show her this vastly fetching creation of pink muslin with gold frogs."

# Chapter Three

The sad fact was that Miss Ann Worthy was in the same state as a schoolboy who, having strained every brain cell to pass a difficult exam, and having succeeded, abandons all further academic effort.

For Miss Worthy had worked long and hard to bring Lord Andrew up to the mark. She had diligently studied reports of the war and of politics in the newspapers, although she was completely uninterested in either. She had paid several guineas of her pin money to a Latin scholar to write a little Latin poem for her and coach her in pronunciation so that she could startle the handsome lord with her erudition and wit. Although she preferred to wear all the latest extravagances of dress from damped and near-transparent muslin to headdresses of fifteen feathers all dyed different colors, she had, on the advice of a top dressmaker, modified her dress to suit her years and status, although she felt sure it did not become her in the least. But Lord Andrew, she knew, was a martinet with very precise ideas of what ladies should wear and how ladies should behave. She had made a study of him before she had actually been introduced to him.

Now the "exams" were over. She had won her

lord. An engagement between two such well-bred members of society was just about as binding as a wedding.

Flushed with triumph and being possessed of a good deal of personal vanity, Miss Worthy quite forgot that she had not appeared to be very attractive to men before her engagement and became convinced she was a diamond of the first water.

The weather, which had turned fine just after Miss Mortimer's arrival in town, stayed that way. London was a pretty sight with all the fine clothes and jewelry on show and windows of ballrooms open to let in the balmy air.

While Penelope Mortimer endured being pinned and fitted for gown after gown, Lord Andrew squired his fiancée to various events. He considered her dress was becoming most unflattering but felt it impolite to say so. In the past, when a lady's attire or manner had displeased him, he had simply made a point of steering away from her. But he was engaged to Miss Worthy, and so he decided to indulge her odd tastes until they were married, by which time she would have promised before God and man to obey him.

It was the way she had begun to ogle other men and then claim that they were smitten with her that grated more than anything else.

At the opera ball or at Almack's Assembly rooms she would flash bold glances in the direction of some newcomer to society and then whisper to Lord Andrew, "Only see how that dreadful man stares at me! I wish he would not. I declare the gentlemen never realize how their bold looks terrify us weak females so!"

Had Lord Andrew had any high opinion of women, then a week of this would have been enough to give him a violent disgust of his fiancée, but he rated the fair sex as low, weak-minded, clinging creatures who only needed a firm hand.

But no doubt had Miss Worthy gone on be-having in this way for much longer, then even Lord Andrew might have seriously begun to con-sider ways to break the engagement. Help was to come from an unexpected quarter. After a week, Penelope's new gowns, slaved over into the night by a row of seamstresses, were ready, and she made her debut. Penelope Mortimer was the one who was going to send Miss Worthy back to her studies.

Lord Andrew had considered removing himself from his parents' home, for his mother's odd behavior had given him a resentment of her which clung in his mind like a burr. But for all her faults, the duchess knew how to run a beau-tiful, charming home, and so he was reluctant to leave, particularly as accommodation was hard to find at any price once the Season had begun.

The duchess was expert at flower arrangements and at the clever use of colors and fabrics. Having no feeling for servants at all, she treated them like pieces of machinery and saw that they were well oiled with plenty of good food and were kept in tip-top running condition.

And so he continued to stay. He did not see Penelope at all during that week after the disastrous visit to the Tower of London.

Then his mother summoned him. He eyed her rather warily now, hoping she would not do any of those strange things like scream at him or faint.

"Andrew," said the duchess, "tonight is Penelope's debut."

He mentally checked his own social calendar. "The Dempseys' ball, I presume?"

"Yes. You attend, of course. Shall you be fetching Miss Worthy?"

"Not tonight. Miss Worthy said she might be late, and I agreed to meet her there."

"Good. In that case little Penelope and myself will be glad of your escort."

"So long as you do not expect me to dance attendance on Miss Mortimer once we are there."

"Well, you know, Andrew, I do think you might stand up with her for two dances. Your engagement has been announced in the newspapers, and so everyone knows you are shackled to Miss Worthy."

"Are you sure," said Lord Andrew, "that Miss Mortimer knows how to go on in society? Has she had any training?"

"She does not need any. She looks so beautiful."

Lord Andrew only remembered Penelope as being pretty.

"I hope," he said cautiously, "that you are not going to force me to entertain Miss Mortimer during the Season?"

"No. After tonight she will have beaux aplenty and will have no need of you."

Lord Andrew took particular pains over his dress that evening. He felt he was putting on armor to protect him from the social gaffes he felt sure Miss Mortimer was bound to commit. His black hair was brushed and pomaded until it shone with blue lights. The white sculpture of his cravat rose above the trim line of a green and gold striped waistcoat. His coat of raven black and his black silk knee breeches and white stockings with gold clocks all appeared molded to his tall, athletic body.

He dabbed some perfume behind his ears, picked up his bicorne, his gloves, and his fan, and made his way downstairs, grateful that the fashion for men carrying enormous muffs had been "exploded" — the cant for out of fashion.

He had drunk several glasses of wine before his mother creaked into the drawing room over an hour late, her little crumpled face flushed with a high color caused by the wicked constriction of her corsets. She looked like one of those nests of Russian wooden dolls where the head of one has been removed, leaving the thick outer body of the first doll with the smaller head of the second doll poking out of it.

He glanced pointedly at the clock on the mantel and asked, "Where is Miss Mortimer?"

"Penelope should just be descending the stairs. Let us go."

Mother and son went out into the hall. Lord Andrew looked up. Penelope was indeed just descending the staircase.

Her fair, silvery hair was crowned with a coronet of pink and white roses. Her gown was of rose pink, criss-crossed with threads of gold to make a diamond pattern. The neckline was low. The sleeves had been slashed like a Renaissance gown.

He thought in a dazed way that she looked like an illustration to one of the stories by the Brothers Grimm.

It was almost a relief when the new fairy-tale Penelope said in a practical voice, "I was dressed an hour ago, but I gather it is the fashion to be deliberately late and so make an appearance."

"You look so very beautiful, Miss Mortimer," he said gallantly, "that you do not need to do anything to attract attention to yourself."

"Thank you," said Penelope. He took her cloak from her arm and put it about her shoulders.

The butler hurried to open the street door.

Lord Andrew frowned as he saw his mother's landau waiting outside. "An open carriage!" he exclaimed.

"Yes, an open carriage," said the duchess. "Everyone will see us."

"Are you not afraid the mob might spit on you?" asked Lord Andrew.

There had not been a revolution in England as there had been in France, but members of the proletariat often roamed the streets of the West

End and would jeer and catcall at the aristocracy as they went out for the evening's amusements.

"We have two outriders," said the duchess placidly, "and you, dear Andrew, will protect us."

But Penelope's beauty, Lord Andrew discovered, was not the kind to excite envy in the bosom of the ordinary people. Rather it drew gasps of wonder and admiration. When their carriage stopped for a moment in the press of traffic, passersby stood on the pavement and stared open-mouthed with pleased smiles on their faces, rather like so many poor children looking at a beautiful doll in a toy shop window.

Penelope appeared very calm, but inside she was frightened to death. She was now appalled at the amount of money that had been spent on her clothes. What if she was not a success? The duchess would be furious. Oh, beautiful cottage in Lower Bexham, where she planned to improve the garden during the lazy summer days — where she could be her own mistress!

She gazed down unseeingly into the admiring eyes of the populace and wished she could spring down from the carriage and run away.

Lord and Lady Dempsey's house had a deceptively narrow frontage which led to enormous rooms once you were inside. It was all glittering and bewildering to Penelope as they passed between a line of footmen in red and gold livery with gold dress swords lining either side of the staircase which soared from the hall of black and gold tiles. The most enormous chandelier

46

Penelope had ever seen blazed overhead — and she could see it, the chandelier being far enough away.

Miss Worthy had made a late arrival, but Penelope's entrance came half an hour after her own.

Until that moment, Miss Worthy had been feeling very well satisfied with her own appearance. She had not been asked to dance but had assumed that every man in the room longed for her company but respected the fact that she was now Lord Andrew's property. Her near-transparent white muslin was worn over an invisible petticoat. She was wearing fifteen multicolored plumes as a headdress.

Her eyes dropped from the tall figure of her fiancé to the smaller figure of Penelope at his side — Penelope, who was causing a ripple of admiring comment to run along the row of chaperones. Her dress was nothing out of the way, thought Miss Worthy, staring at the rose pink gown embroidered with gold. The duchess led Penelope over to where Mrs. Blenkinsop was seated. Lord Andrew looked about the room, saw Miss Worthy, and crossed the floor, bowed to her mother, who was seated next to her, and sat down on Miss Worthy's other side.

"Who is that odd female with the dyed hair who came in with you?" asked Miss Worthy.

"Miss Penelope Mortimer, a protégée of my mother. She is but lately come to town, and she does not dye her hair."

"Indeed!" said Miss Worthy. "Such an odd, unfashionable color. Do you not think so, Mama?"

And Mrs. Worthy, who on seeing Penelope had sent up a prayer of thanks that her daughter was engaged to Lord Andrew, and that there was therefore nothing to fear from this dazzler, said stoutly, "Yes, it looks false. Quite like spun glass."

"I am surprised the dear duchess could not persuade the chit to wear white," said Miss Worthy, waving a large fan of osprey feathers.

"The dress was my mother's choice," said Lord Andrew. "I think it a delightful creation, simple and modest."

"It is cut too low for such a young girl. She is showing too much neck," said Miss Worthy. Her fan tickled his nose, and he turned his head away in irritation. He looked across to where Penelope was now sitting with his mother. The neckline of her dress just exposed the tops of two firm white breasts.

"Perhaps," he said, for he was suddenly out of charity with Miss Mortimer for looking so seductive when his fiancée seemed hell-bent on appearing as the female of some barbaric tribe.

Miss Worthy smiled. "I am glad you are come, for that terrible rake, Mr. Barcourt, is here, and no woman is safe with him."

Lord Andrew looked across to where Mr. John Barcourt was standing with a group of friends. Barcourt was a fine figure of a man with hair almost as fair as Penelope's own. He had a dreamy, romantic expression. Lord Andrew did not think him a rake but only a highly susceptible man who fell violently in love at least three times during the Season.

"Has he been troubling you?" he asked.

"He has not dared come near, for all the world knows I am engaged to you," said Miss Worthy. "But such scorching looks as he has sent in this direction! Is that not so, Mama?"

"Yes, my love," said Mrs. Worthy dutifully.

Penelope was glad the ballroom was so large. Although the people near her were little more than a colored blur, she could clearly make out the faces and dress of the guests on the other side of the ballroom. Her wide blue gaze fell on Mr. Barcourt. She looked at the London Season's famous heartbreaker and thought he reminded her of that desperately handsome boy who worked in the butcher's shop in Lower Bexham: handsome but weak.

The duchess meanwhile was narrowly watching the progression of her friend, Mrs. Blenkinsop, round the ballroom. Mrs. Blenkinsop was gossiping busily, and eyes were turned in Penelope's direction.

Fiddle, thought the duchess angrily. She is out to sabotage me. She is telling them all that Penelope is merely another of my lame ducks and has no dowry whatsoever. Her gaze shifted to the young lady who sat next to her on the other side from Penelope. Miss Amy Tilney was

Mrs. Blenkinsop's niece, a plain, shy wisp of a thing. But Maria Blenkinsop had already let it be known the girl was possessed of a comfortable dowry. Her eyes took on a hard, stubborn look. She would not be defeated by Mrs. Blenkinsop.

"Do change places with me, Miss Tilney," said the duchess, "and chat to Penelope. I am desirous to talk to Mrs. Partridge." Amy changed places and sat next to Penelope while the duchess smiled sweetly on Mrs. Partridge, London's biggest gossip.

"And how is the world with you?" asked Mrs. Partridge.

"The world goes very badly," sighed the duchess. "But I shall not live to see much more of it."

Mrs. Partridge nearly fell off her chair with excitement. "My dear duchess," she cried, "never tell me you are ill."

"Gravely ill," said the duchess. "I do not think I shall live much beyond the end of the Season. Do you know Mr. Anderson, the royal doctor? He tells me I have the Blasted Wasting."

"Gracious! What is that?" asked Mrs. Partridge, eyeing the duchess's well-upholstered figure.

"A rare disease brought from the Indies," said the duchess with a dismissive wave of her hand.

"Then you should be home in bed."

"My duty lies with little Penelope here. It must be well known that I am to leave my vast personal fortune to her, and I would see her safely launched and protected from adventurers before I . . . die."

"Is this your first Season?" Amy was asking Penelope timidly.

"Yes, and I hope my last," said Penelope gloomily.

"Oh, yes, it will be your last," said Amy simply. "You are so very pretty, you will be wed quite soon."

"I do not want to be wed at all," said Penelope, taking a liking to this girl although she could not quite see her, but warming to the friendly interest in her voice. "I want to be left alone."

"I know what you mean," said Amy in a low voice, "but it is not possible for such as we. We have no free will."

"Oh, yes we have," said Penelope. "No one can stop us thinking what we want to think. And it is always possible to plot and plan a way out of any predicament."

"Here is Mr. Barcourt approaching us," said Amy with a hint of longing in her voice. "He is so very handsome."

"May I have the pleasure of this dance?" said Mr. Barcourt, bowing low before Penelope. But as Penelope could not quite make him out and assumed somehow that he and Amy were acquainted, she also assumed he was asking Amy to dance. So she smiled and said to Amy, "There you are, and off you go, Miss Tilney. Your first dance of the evening."

Somehow there was nothing Mr. Barcourt

could do but take Amy onto the floor. At his invitation, Penelope had not looked at him once but had immediately turned to Amy Tilney.

Then Penelope suddenly found herself being besieged on all sides to dance. She picked the first one who had asked her and went out to join a set being made up for a country dance.

She found that dance a great strain, for her weak eyesight put her constantly in danger of losing her partner. She hoped once the dance was over that she would be allowed to go back to her chair and sit quietly. But no sooner had it finished and no sooner had she dropped gracefully down into a curtsy than she was besieged again by a group of gentlemen.

In another part of the ballroom, Lord Andrew was being hailed by his closest friend, a Scotsman called Mr. Ian Macdonald. Mr. Macdonald was as messy and careless as Lord Andrew was precise and correct. Where Lord Andrew's tailored clothes flattered his athletic figure, Mr. Macdonald's were either too tight or too loose. He had a huge, beefy face, small, clever brown eyes like a bear, and a mop of glossy brown curls.

"My good friend," Mr. Macdonald hailed Lord Andrew. "Why did you not tell me the dreadful news? Perhaps I could have been of some comfort."

"What terrible news?" demanded Lord Andrew acidly, for he feared his friend might be referring to his engagement. Lord Andrew glanced to where his fiancée was now dancing with a thin young army captain. One of her feathers was dropping down her back, and a good part of the revelation of her charms which should have been saved for the marriage bed was being displayed through damped muslin at a London ball. He felt, nonetheless, that his distaste at her appearance was overly severe. Many of the ladies were wearing just as little, and it was an age when they stopped posting guards at the opera to keep the prostitutes out, for the guards kept arresting ladies of the ton, not being able to tell the difference.

"Come over here and sit down," said Mr. Macdonald. He led the way behind a potted palm to where a sofa had been placed against the wall.

"I lost my own mother last year, as you know," began Mr. Macdonald in a low voice. "I cried for weeks, I can tell you. Still miss her." He gave a hiccuping sort of sob and pulled a large handkerchief from the pocket in his tails and dabbed his eyes.

"I know your grief must still bite deep, Ian," said Lord Andrew, who had long envied his friend his closeness with his family. He rose and stepped behind the palms and told a footman to fetch them two glasses of wine, and then returned to his friend.

"Talk about your grief, Ian," said Lord Andrew. "I was supposed to dance attendance on my mother's new lame duck, but she is such a success, I cannot get near her. So I have plenty of time to listen to you."

"I'm not talking about my mother," said Ian Macdonald. "I'm talking about yours."

"Mine! There is nothing up with her."

"Oh, my dear friend. That I should be the first to tell you! The Duchess of Parkworth has" — his voice sank to a mournful whisper — "the Blasted Wasting."

"Never heard of it."

"A rare disease from the Indies."

"Dammit, man, does my mother look as if she's wasting away? Who is putting about such a farrago of lies?"

"Not lies. For that gossip Partridge had it direct from the duchess herself. And there is worse."

"Can there be?" demanded Lord Andrew cynically.

"She says she is going to leave her personal fortune to that chit, Penelope Mortimer."

The footman appeared with a bottle of wine and two glasses. Lord Andrew ordered him to leave the whole bottle. When he had poured out two glasses, handed one to Ian, drained his own in one gulp, and refilled it, he said, "Ian, the situation is this. My mother is competing with Mrs. Blenkinsop. Mrs. Blenkinsop is bringing out her niece, Miss Tilney. Miss Tilney does not rate highly in the looks department but has a sizable fortune. Miss Mortimer has none. Mrs. Blenkinsop, I know, has already been gossiping to the effect that Miss Mortimer is one of Mother's lame ducks, of no fortune or breeding. But before that acid began to bite, I assume my mother told all those barefaced lies to Mrs. Partridge. Hence Penelope Mortimer's success."

"You are sure?"

"Oh, quite."

"But Miss Mortimer is divinely beautiful, is she not?"

"She is very well in her way," said Lord Andrew repressively. He stood up and peered through the palms. "Strange," he said over his shoulder. "She is nowhere in sight. You will keep this to yourself, Ian, but it is my belief that Miss Mortimer is a trifle simple. I hope she has not done anything silly. Perhaps I had better go to look for her. But make yourself easy on the matter of my mother's death. I am sure she will live a great many years longer. In a few weeks, the novelty of Miss Mortimer will have worn off, and that is the last anyone will hear of her."

Lord Andrew diligently searched the ballroom, the card room, and the supper room. There was no sign of Penelope. His mother appeared at his elbow looking agitated and whispered that Penelope had said she was going off to refresh her appearance, but servants sent to the dressing room for the ladies had reported she was not there.

"You had best not rouse an alarm," said Lord Andrew. "I shall find her, and later we must talk of my mother's so-called forthcoming death."

He went out onto the landing and looked over the banister and searched the hall with his eyes.

No Penelope. The dressing rooms for the guests to repair their toilet were on the floor above the ballroom. He made his way up there quite forgetting he was engaged to dance the cotillion with Miss Worthy.

Penelope was standing in a small, weedy enclosed bit of garden at the back of the house, wondering what on earth to do. She had been reluctant to return to the hot ballroom and had wandered downstairs and through the hall to the back and then along a little passage to an open door at the end. She had walked through it and found herself in the little garden. The air was sweet and warm, and a full moon silvered the tall weeds, making them look like magical plants.

Then some servant had slammed the door shut, Penelope had found it locked. Above her head, the loud noise of the orchestra drowned out her frantic knockings.

She raised her skirts and took her precious spectacles out of a pocket in her petticoat and popped them on her nose.

She was now thoroughly terrified of what the duchess's rage would be like if she stayed missing for much longer. A long black drainpipe rose up the back of the building, and one of its arms shooting out at right angles was right under an open window on the second floor where Penelope remembered the dressing rooms to be.

She could easily climb that drainpipe, but her gown would be ruined, that gown which had cost so much money.

Penelope decided frantically that if she removed her dress and slung it round her neck and climbed up in her petticoat, she could dive into the dressing room, pop on her gown, and run down to the ballroom. Shivering with nerves, she put her spectacles back in her petticoat pocket, untied the tapes of her gown and took it off, and then tied it around her neck.

Lord Andrew became convinced Penelope was in the ladies' dressing room, probably hidden behind a screen. This glittering social event had probably been too much for such a country-bred miss. There was surely no other logical place she could be. He sent one of the maids in to search thoroughly, but the maid returned and said there was no one there.

Lord Andrew handed her a crown and told her to stand guard outside while he looked himself.

He went in, glad that no ladies seemed to want to make repairs at that moment, and looked everywhere. But it was a fairly small room, and it was obvious there was nowhere Penelope could hide.

He was about to leave when he heard strange noises coming from outside the window. He leaned out of the open window and looked down, and then clutched the sill hard.

Pulling herself up the drainpipe, clad in a white petticoat, flesh-colored stockings, and the most frivolous pair of rose-embroidered garters Lord Andrew had ever seen, came Penelope Mortimer.

He darted to the dressing room door, locked

it, ran back to the window, and leaned down to catch Penelope's arm as she came within reach.

She let out a cry of terror and lost her hold, but he had her safe. He pulled her up and then helped her in the window.

"Dress yourself," he said, turning his back on her.

Blushing furiously, Penelope slipped the gown over her head and then asked him in a trembling voice to help her tie her tapes.

He swung about and fastened the tapes and then put his hands on her shoulders. "We must get out of here before anyone comes," he whispered. "I shall talk to you later."

He straightened her headdress, seized a washcloth and roughly scrubbed a smudge of soot from her nose, and then scrubbed her dirty hands.

He unlocked the door and led her out. "Miss Mortimer had fainted," he said severely to the startled maid, "but here is a guinea for you, for you did your best."

He tucked Penelope's arm firmly in his own and led her down to the ballroom.

Miss Worthy saw them arrive. She was furious and frightened. An acid-tongued friend of her mother's had told Miss Worthy that she looked like a harlot and that if she was not careful, The Perfect Gentleman might decide to ditch her in favor of that Mortimer chit, thereby keeping his mother's money in the family.

So to Lord Andrew's relief, after he had delivered Penelope to his mother, he found a meek and ladylike fiancée who had reduced her feathered headdress by eight plumes and who had allowed her damped muslin to dry. To her questions, he replied tersely that Miss Mortimer had fainted and that he had had to rescue her and that Miss Mortimer was the most tiresome idiot it had ever been his ill luck to come across.

"Perhaps," ventured Miss Worthy, "I could set her an example as to manners. She has not had the social training of a member of the ton."

"If you could be a friend to her," said Lord Andrew, "that would indeed be very noble of you. Miss Mortimer needs to be guided by some lady nearer her years."

"Then I shall call on her tomorrow," said Miss Worthy, privately deciding it would be as well to get to know as much about this new enemy as possible.

"You are very good," said Lord Andrew. He gave her a sweet smile and led her to the floor.

# Chapter Four

Lord Andrew meant to tackle his mother again on the subject of Miss Mortimer, but the duchess was so flushed with success over Penelope's triumph that he decided to leave it for the moment.

Penelope, on the other hand, must be spoken to immediately.

They settled down over the tea tray in the drawing room before going to bed. The duchess regaled her husband, who had not been present at the ball, with every detail from the sour look on Mrs. Blenkinsop's face to the name of every gentleman who had danced with Penelope.

"But why were you absent for so long?" demanded the duchess at last.

"As I told you, Your Grace," said Penelope, stifling a yawn, "I fainted." Penelope had decided the easiest course was to adopt Lord Andrew's lie.

"Fainted!" said the duchess awfully. "F-a-i-n-t-e-d," she added, drawling out the word. "I did not say anything when you told me at the ball, but I am convinced you did nothing of the sort, Penelope. This sensibility business is not the fashion it was, and I trust you have not begun to put on airs. You felt a trifle dizzy and exaggerated it into a faint, did you not?"

"Yes, Your Grace," said Penelope, too tired to argue.

"Just as I thought," said the duchess, who had no desire to sponsor a flawed beauty. "Now, you must go to bed and refresh yourself for the morrow, for, if I am not mistaken, we can expect many callers."

Lord Andrew cleared his throat. "I have asked Miss Worthy to call. I am sure her example would be beneficial to Miss Mortimer."

"Fiddlesticks. I do not want Penelope to learn how to dress like a Cyprian or to start parading about with a head full of feathers."

"Mama! Miss Worthy's dress this evening may have been a trifle unfortunate . . ."

"Very unfortunate."

"But Miss Mortimer stands in need of social training."

"All that will happen," said the duchess with relish, "is that Miss Worthy will have her nose put out of joint by all my Penelope's admirers."

"As Miss Worthy is engaged to me, she is in no need of admirers or to be jealous of any other woman."

"That must be just about the most pompous remark I have ever heard," said Penelope.

"Don't sit there glaring, Andrew," said his mother. "Penelope, off to your room."

Penelope gained her room with a sigh of relief. She had walked over to the toilet table to begin her preparations for bed when there was a knock at the door.

"Enter," she called, wondering why Perkins should knock at the door, a thing good servants never did.

Lord Andrew came in.

"Now, Miss Mortimer," he said, "explain what happened this evening."

The little French clock on the mantel chimed four in the morning. "Yesterday evening," corrected Penelope gloomily.

"Very well. Yesterday evening."

Penelope sat down wearily in front of the lace-draped toilet table, raised her arms, and unpinned her headdress.

"It was a chapter of accidents," she said. "I did go to the dressing room. Then I went back down past the ballroom to the hall. I wanted to walk about for a bit. The ballroom was hot, and I was tired of the effort of dancing." Penelope meant she was tired of the effort of remembering her place in the sets when she could not see very well. "There was a door open at the back of the hall. I went through and found myself in a neglected bit of garden. The air was pleasant," she said dreamily. "Then some servant slammed the door and locked it. The orchestra in the ballroom struck up, and no one could hear my bangings and shoutings. I thought if I removed my gown so that it would not be soiled and climbed up the drainpipe to the dressing room, where the window was open, that I might be able to put on my dress and go down to the ballroom, and no one would be any the wiser. But all's well that ends well. I told your mother I had fainted. I am unhurt." She yawned and rubbed her eyes with her knuckles.

"For your own good, and for my mother's good, you cannot go on making social gaffes," said Lord Andrew. "I urge you to attend to Miss Worthy's advice."

Penelope had had a very good view of Miss Worthy when that lady had been dancing far enough away from her.

"I am not used to London ways," said Penelope primly, "nor can I adopt the extremes of dress. It is all very well for a lady of Miss Worthy's mature years, but in a young virgin, it would be damned as fast."

"Miss Worthy, like most ladies, is sometimes given to odd mistakes in dress," said Lord Andrew angrily — angry because the more he thought about his fiancée's gown, the more shocking it seemed. "But she is the epitome of elegance and social deportment most of the time."

"What Her Grace needs," said Penelope half to herself, "is another lame duck."

"I beg your pardon!"

"I wish your mother would find another interest," said Penelope in a stronger voice, "and preferably an interest who takes the same size in gown as I. Were it not for my horror at the amount of money that has already been spent on me, I would run off to the country and risk the duchess's wrath. What is my behavior to you, in any case, Lord Andrew? I am Her Grace's protégée, not yours."

"Then if you wish me to keep out of your affairs," said Lord Andrew angrily, "do not embroil me in them by walking into lions' dens or climbing up drainpipes half naked."

"I was not half naked. Believe me, my lord, in my petticoat, I still concealed more than your fiancée did with her ballgown."

"You are an impertinent little girl. How dare you speak to me so?"

"How dare *you* speak to *me* so!" retaliated Penelope. "Oh, *do* run along. I am so very tired."

"There is just one thing," he said, "before I leave you, which needs explanation. In order to compete with Mrs. Blenkinsop, my mother has seen fit to put it about that she has a deathly illness and she is going to leave her money to you. I trust you do not believe such rubbish."

"No," said Penelope. "Of course not. But there is one thing I have to say to you. It could be argued that neither Her Grace nor Miss Worthy appear to have behaved at the ball with ladylike decorum, the one telling rank lies and the other indecorously gowned, so I do not know why you are standing in the middle of my bedroom giving me a jaw-me-dead."

There was a scratching at the door, and Perkins walked into the room and stopped short at the sight of Lord Andrew.

"I am just going," he said crossly, suiting the action to the words.

A few minutes later his valet struggled to assist a master who kept muttering and cursing under his breath. His valet, Pomfret, was breathlessly saving up every curse and wild gesture to describe to the upper servants the next day. Pomfret had been hired as a valet to Lord Andrew just before the beginning of the previous Season. Hitherto, he had found the work boring. Lord Andrew's impeccable manners and impeccable dress gave Pomfret nothing to work on. His correct politeness with equals and servants gave the gossip-starved Pomfret nothing to talk about. Now it looked as if Lord Andrew was either drunk or about to suffer from a nervous breakdown. The valet handed his master his nightcap and his glass of warm wine and water and looked forward to a rosier future.

That lie, which had been so useful to the duchess the evening before, turned out to be the wreck of her plans for the following day.

She had quite forgotten about it and was mortified to find that the gentlemen who had danced with Penelope had not called in person. Mute witness to this was in the array of unbent cards in the silver tray in the hall. Gentlemen or ladies who had called in person always turned down one corner. Certainly one had sent a love poem — the duchess considered it her right to open Penelope's post — and another two, bunches of flowers.

It was only when Miss Worthy arrived and began to speak to the duchess in a hushed whisper, and occasionally pressing that lady's hand, that the duchess found out the truth of the matter.

"No callers at all," the duchess complained.

"I am here, dear Mama-in-law," mourned Miss Worthy.

"Stop calling me by that stupid name. You aren't married yet, and if you go about flaunting yourself in damped muslin for much longer, you won't be."

At that Miss Worthy began to cry. "No need to take on so," said the duchess impatiently. "Andrew's shackled to you, and there's an end of it."

Miss Worthy raised streaming eyes. Penelope, sitting a little way away from the couple, wrinkled her nose. There was an odd smell of onion in the drawing room.

"It is your courageous behavior which quite goes to my heart," said Miss Worthy, who had learned the story of the duchess's doom from her parents and had not yet had a chance to discuss it with Lord Andrew.

"Stop crying. *I'm* the one who should be crying. I have a weak heart," said the duchess crossly.

"I know. I know," wailed Miss Worthy. She flashed a look at Penelope, who was sitting looking out of the bow window at the trees in the park. "I am shocked at you, Miss Mortimer," said Miss Worthy. "Some show of distress, some sensibility, would be more becoming in you."

"I hope Penelope knows better than to cry and bawl because she hasn't any callers," said the duchess. "Where's Andrew? Was ever a woman so plagued."

"I am talking about the Blasted Wasting."

"The Blasted what? I distinctly heard you snigger, Penelope. Mind your manners."

"The Blasted Wasting," said Miss Worthy. "You know, that disease from the Indies."

"Oh, that," said the duchess. "Oh, fiddle. Oh, damme. So that's why no one has called! I have not got the blasted anything, Miss Worthy, so you may dry your eyes. It was some malice put about by Maria Blenkinsop because she's jealous of Penelope, only having a Friday-faced antidote to puff off herself."

"I thought Miss Tilney charming," said Penelope.

"And who asked your opinion, miss? I must make calls. I must scotch this rumor. Andrew!" she cried as her son's tall figure entered the room. "Do take Miss Worthy away somewhere . . . anywhere. I know, take her for a drive in the park, and take Miss Mortimer with you."

Miss Worthy was wearing an elegant carriage dress of gray alpaca with a black velvet collar. On her head was a stylish shako. Her appearance put Lord Andrew in a good humor.

"I must change," said Penelope. "I won't be long."

She reappeared a bare quarter of an hour later in a carriage dress of green velvet piped with gold braid. A grass green velvet hat shaped like a man's beaver was tilted at a rakish angle on her curls. She looked breathtakingly lovely.

"You must speak to your mama about Miss Mortimer's dress," whispered Miss Worthy to Lord Andrew while Penelope was making her farewells to the duchess.

"Yes, I shall," he said curtly. "That dressmaker she found for Penelope is a genius."

So the three left together in a bad mood. Lord Andrew was cross because he felt Penelope had deliberately gone out of her way to outshine Miss Worthy, Penelope did not like Miss Worthy and had spent a long and tedious day waiting for those gentlemen callers who never came, and Miss Worthy was furious because Lord Andrew had refused to criticize Penelope's dress.

He drove them in his phaeton, Miss Worthy on his left and Penelope on his right. By the time they had driven a certain way into the park, Lord Andrew realized with a shock that he was behaving very badly indeed. It was not like him to indulge in a bout of bad temper and forget his social duty.

"You must forgive me, Miss Worthy," he said, "but I fear I have been put sadly out of temper by family problems."

Miss Worthy saw a way to score. "*Iris furorus brevis est,* is it not, Miss Mortimer?"

"I think you mean *Ira furor brevis est* — anger is short madness," said Penelope. "Do you read much Horace, Miss Worthy?"

"Yes, all the time," said Miss Worthy grimly.

"I prefer novels," said Penelope.

"That does not surprise me."

"Indeed, Miss Worthy. Why?"

"Most young ladies addle their minds with such rubbish."

"I would not call them all rubbish and dismiss them so. Have you read Miss Austen's *Sense and Sensibility*?"

"Of course not. Have I not just explained? I have no time for such frivolities."

"Oh, you should," said Penelope. "It would quite convert you."

Miss Worthy abandoned the subject of literature and then proceeded to try to score with art.

"Oh, stop!" she cried.

Lord Andrew reined in his horses. Miss Worthy raised her gloved hands and formed them into a square. "The perspective," she murmured. "See, over there where the guards have stationed their horses under that stand of trees. What symmetry!" She closed her eyes.

Penelope, who had excellent long sight, gazed interestedly across the park to see what had entranced Miss Worthy.

The guards on their horses ceased to be picturesque, for one of them, having drunk too long and too well, leaned over his saddle and "cascaded" into the bushes.

"How very moving," murmured Miss Worthy, her eyes still closed.

"I agree with you," said Penelope with a snort

of laughter. "I should think that poor guardsman has *moved* most of his insides."

Miss Worthy's eyes flew open. The guards were riding off. What on earth did Miss Mortimer mean? And why had Lord Andrew begun to laugh?

She decided not to ask but sat with her back ramrod straight and her face set in a disapproving look.

It was just as well. For Lord Andrew would have been hard put to explain why he found it all so funny. But it had touched a chord of the ridiculous in him which he had not known he possessed. He had never laughed at anything silly before and did not know why he could barely control himself.

Somehow the day had become sharp and crystal-bright. Everything was new and green and fresh, and he felt more alive than he had ever done in his life before.

Although he soon had his outburst of laughter well under control, the strange elation remained with him, bubbling and chuckling inside like a brook running over the pebbles.

He then began to wonder what really went on inside Miss Mortimer's beautiful head and lurked behind those vacant eyes. She could quote Horace, and she had made Miss Worthy's artistic posturing quite ridiculous. He gazed down at her with a new awareness in his eyes, but Penelope only saw a blur of his face turned in her direction and dutifully smiled.

The breeze lifted a tendril of her silver-fair hair, and her wide eyes were as blue and innocent as the sky above. He felt a queer little tug at his heart as he looked at her. She did not belong in London society, and he felt, were she to remain much longer, she might become spoiled. She would soon learn not to indulge in saying exactly what she thought. He decided the best thing he could do would be to try to help her to get her wish by returning her to the country.

This thought preoccupied him on the road back. He drove Miss Worthy to her home and then returned to Park Street with Penelope. She did not say anything as they drove through the streets but contented herself with staring off into the distance. Lord Andrew did not know that Penelope, as her long sight was good, was contenting herself by looking at all she could see.

"I would like a word with you, Miss Mortimer," he said as they entered the house.

"Another lecture," sighed Penelope.

"No," he said. "Perhaps I might be able to help you."

The duchess, he learned from the butler, was still out on her calls, and the duke had gone to his club.

He led her into the drawing room and asked if she would like tea. Penelope said she would, so he waited until the tea tray had been brought in, said yes, he took sugar, and then watched in amazement as Penelope proceeded to pour tea into the sugar bowl.

"I do not like my tea very sweet," he said.

"I have not yet given you any sugar, my lord."

"On the contrary, you have just filled the sugar bowl with tea."

"How silly of me," said Penelope. "Now what shall I do?"

He rang the bell, ordered another bowl of sugar, and then, when it had arrived, busied himself with the tea things.

"You puzzle me," he said. "How comes it that a lady who can quote Horace does quite mad things like filling up the sugar bowl with tea?"

Pride kept Penelope from telling the truth. Had not her parents always said that ladies who had to wear spectacles never attracted gentlemen and that it was best to conceal one's defect until one was married? But you don't want to get married! said a cross little voice in Penelope's head, but she ignored it and said aloud, "I am absent-minded, I fear. What did you wish to talk to me about?"

"I am persuaded you would really be much happier in the country. To that end, I am prepared to talk to my mother again."

Penelope took a delicate sip of tea. "All you will do is provoke the most dreadful scene. I am still a novelty, you know. Give it a few weeks and you will find Her Grace beginning to tire."

The door of the drawing room opened, the duke poked his head around it, saw them, and muttered something about going to the library.

"You are very cynical," said Lord Andrew. "Would you not like to wed? That is the whole purpose of a Season."

"No, I would not," said Penelope. "Your mother will have explained her lies away. Everyone will now know I have no money or any expectations of it. I cannot hope for a rich husband; therefore I should not have the comfort of being separated from him the way I would were I to command a large establishment. A rich husband is always on the hunting field, at his club, or in Parliament. One need not see much of him. A husband with modest means is always underfoot, or so I have observed. I am not prepared to spend the rest of my life with someone I do not like just for the sake of becoming married. Now, in your case, as you are, or so I learned, greatly interested in agriculture, Miss Worthy will not have to see much of you."

"What on earth, my impertinent Miss Mortimer, gives you the impression that my fiancée does not dote on my company?"

"She is not in love with you, nor you with her."

He sighed. "Those pernicious novels! I have seen respectable girls running off with footmen, and all for love. I have seen young men marrying portionless girls of little breeding, and all for love. Their marriages always end in disaster. Love is no basis for marriage. Equal breeding, similar tastes, and similar interests are the bedrock of any relationship."

"Perhaps for such as you," said Penelope. "But in my case, I shall marry for love or not at all, which probably means not at all. But I shall have my independence and hard work to keep me occupied. I have discovered a gift for gardening. I grow very fine vegetables, I assure you."

"What kind of soil do you have?"

"Clay soil. Very heavy."

"And what do you use?"

"Lime to break it down and sweeten it, and then I find that horse manure is a great fertilizer, and to be had for nothing. One simply goes out in the roads with a shovel."

Lord Andrew blinked at the idea of this fairylike creature searching the country roads with a brush and shovel. "What an undignified picture you conjure up!" he exclaimed.

"Ah, but as my own mistress, I do not have to care about dignity or the lack of it. There seems to be a great deal of toing and froing downstairs. Perhaps you have callers."

"Then no doubt someone will let me know if anyone wants to see me."

"More tea?" asked Penelope, picking up the pot.

"Yes, I thank you." Lord Andrew grabbed his cup and held it out in time to catch the stream of hot tea which had just been about to descend on his knee. "Are you longsighted by any chance, Miss Mortimer?"

"Not I," said Penelope quickly.

He leaned back in his chair and studied her

thoughtfully. They were to go to the opera that evening. He would study Penelope's face as she watched the opera. He would ask her questions about the costume and the performers, for he was all at once sure she had difficulty in seeing.

The door burst open and the duchess came rushing in, her face mottled with excitement and every stay in her corsets creaking like the timbers of a four-master rounding Cape Horn.

"My dear!" she cried. "Such excitement. Mr. Barcourt is come to ask our leave to pay his addresses to Penelope. He called on Giles when I was out." Giles was her husband, the duke. "I came just in time to add my permission. Such a triumph. Barcourt! Ten thousand a year. Very comfortable and all, just as it ought to be."

"Barcourt cannot be serious," said Lord Andrew testily after a quick look at Penelope's stricken face. "He is always falling in love."

"But he has never proposed to anyone before," said the duchess. "Come quickly, Andrew."

Lord Andrew looked helplessly at Penelope, but she was now sitting sedately in front of the tea tray with her eyes lowered.

"Come, Andrew," repeated his mother in imperative tones.

He followed her reluctantly from the room.

Penelope waited until the door was closed behind them, opened her reticule, took out her ugly but efficient steel spectacles, and popped them on her nose. She took off her pretty bonnet, put it under her chair, and then combed her hair straight up on top of her head and wound it into a severe knot.

Then she folded her hands and waited.

The door opened and Mr. Barcourt walked in.

# Chapter Five

Mr. Barcourt stopped short on the threshold. For one brief moment he hoped that the young lady facing him would prove to be Penelope's elder sister. The sunlight winked on her thick-lensed spectacles, and her hair was scraped painfully straight up on the top of her head.

To know the character of women was not at all necessary to engender the exquisite pangs of love in Mr. Barcourt's breast. Their looks and his vivid imagination did all that was necessary. He had, therefore, fallen in love with Penelope at the Dempseys' ball. Her vague, dreaming expression combined with her ethereal beauty had prompted him to propose for the first time in his life.

Underneath all his romanticism, there was a practical streak in Mr. Barcourt's nature which had held him back before popping the question. But the intelligence that the duchess was at death's door and about to leave her fortune to this goddess had brought him up to the mark.

His first shock had come when the duke had pooh-poohed the idea of his wife's imminent death. He said bluntly that Penelope was portionless. Mr. Barcourt might have then withdrawn his offer had not the duchess arrived on the scene to say that Penelope would have a dowry of three thousand pounds. It was not much, particularly in the inflationary days of the Regency, but to a man who had thought a moment before that he would have nothing at all, it seemed a splendid sum. He was accordingly given the ducal blessing and told he might have ten minutes alone with Penelope.

"Come in, Mr. Barcourt," said Penelope, "and sit down."

Her voice was rather harsh and had a distinct country burr.

He sat down opposite her. Her eyes seemed smaller than he had remembered behind those awful glasses, and they glittered with sharp intelligence.

He sat dumb, wishing this creature would go away to be replaced with the fairy-tale figure of the ball.

"Would you like tea, sir?" asked Penelope. She had pronounced the "sir" as "zurr," just like the lowest peasant. Mr. Barcourt's love received a death blow.

"Er, yes, Miss Mortimer," he said. "Hot in here," he added, running a finger round the inside of his starched collar.

"I'm sure I hadn't noticed, zurr," drawled Penelope with the dulcet tones of a corncrake. "You'll be wantin' milk and sugar, I s'pose?"

"Yes, I thank you. Do you know why I am come?"

"Oh, yus," said Penelope. "You be wanting to marry me. I'd loik that. I've always wanted childer. Lots and lots. Mrs. Barnes, down in the village, now she got twenty-one, and all hale and hearty."

"Twenty-one!" echoed Mr. Barcourt faintly. His hand holding the cup and saucer began to tremble.

"I was glad to find you had a place in the country," went on Penelope. "For I don't loik the town, and that's a fact. Nothing loik good country air and plain country cooking and hard work in the fields, I always say."

Mr. Barcourt, a perpetually absent landlord who loathed the country and did not even hunt, was terrified. Stark, raving fear animated his wits.

He put his cup and saucer carefully on the table and said in a dazed voice. "Where am I?"

"You're about to propose marriage to me."

"Who you?" demanded Mr. Barcourt in a thin, high voice.

"Me Penelope Mortimer," said Penelope with a huge grin — a peasant grin, thought Mr. Barcourt, and his fastidious soul recoiled.

"I have lost my memory!" cried Mr. Barcourt, jumping to his feet. " 'Sdeath! I do not know where I am or what I am doing. Beg pardon, whoever you are." He scrambled for the door. "Good-bye. Forgive. Not myself. Servant, ma'am." He tumbled out onto the landing and nearly collided with the duke and duchess, who had just approached the door.

"I do not know who I am," wailed Mr. Barcourt. "I have lost my memory."

Lord Andrew came up to join the group. "What is this nonsense, Barcourt?" he said. "You have just proposed marriage to Miss Penelope Mortimer."

"No I haven't," screamed Mr. Barcourt. "Not I. Never propose to anyone. Who are you anyway?"

"We are the Duke and Duchess of Parkworth," said the duchess awfully.

"I'm sick," cried Mr. Barcourt. "I don't know anyone. Don't know what I am saying."

He dived down the steps, and the ducal family stood looking at one another as the street door slammed.

They went into the drawing room. Penelope, her glasses tucked safely back in her reticule, her hat on her loosened curls, sat looking vaguely into the middle distance.

"What on earth happened?" screamed the duchess.

In her usual pleasant voice, free from any accent, Penelope said in a bewildered way, "I do not know. He talked so wildly. I think he is quite mad."

"But did he propose?" shouted the duchess.

"Oh, no, I don't think so," said Penelope, wrinkling her brow. "Let me see; he asked for tea, and then he began to shake and said he did not know who he was. I am vastly cast down, Your Grace, and would like to retire."

"You are not going anywhere, miss, until I get to the bottom of this," howled the duchess. "Oh, to think how I planned to crow over Maria Blenkinsop at the opera tonight! Andrew, you must challenge Barcourt to a duel."

Penelope gave a pathetic little sob.

"Let her go to her room," said Lord Andrew angrily. "Do you not see she has had enough?"

"Very well," said the duchess, suddenly subdued as the full force of her own disappointment hit her.

For half an hour after Penelope had retired, the Parkworth family chewed over the strange behavior of Mr. Barcourt. Lord Andrew urged his mother to set Penelope free and let her go home. But the duchess gradually brightened. "If she can attract such a one as Barcourt," she said slowly, "even though he chose this unfortunate moment to have a brainstorm, then who knows who she might draw into the net."

In vain did Lord Andrew argue the wisdom of letting Penelope go. He finally left his parents and went upstairs to change for dinner.

As he passed Penelope's room, he heard stifled sounds coming from inside.

He was angry with his mother, and he was angry with Penelope for taking the rejection of such a one as Barcourt so hard. He walked a little way away and then went back, opened the door of her room, and walked inside.

She was lying facedown on the bed, her shoulders shaking.

He went over and sat on the edge of the bed and put a comforting hand on her shoulder.

"Come now, Miss Mortimer," he said. "Must I remind you that you said you did not want to marry except for love? And you cannot be in love with Barcourt. You barely know him."

"But he has s-such n-nice legs," came Penelope's muffled voice.

He looked down at her in sudden suspicion, and his grip on her shoulder tightened. He pulled her over on her back.

"You're laughing!" he exclaimed.

"Oh, it w-was s-so funny," giggled Penelope. "All that where-am-I and who-am-I. I wish you could have seen him."

He took her by the shoulders and gave her a shake. "Barcourt showed all the signs of a man about to propose. It was you — you did something to scare him."

"I was myself, I assure you, a good country girl." Penelope let out a snort of laughter.

Lord Andrew became aware of the warmth of the shoulders through the thin muslin of her gown as he held her down on the bed, of her pink lips trembling with laughter, of the tumbled disarray of her glorious hair, and of the wide blue depths of her eyes.

The Perfect Gentlemen leaned down and pressed firm lips against that laughing mouth.

They both stayed very still, pressed against each other, both shocked rigid by the skyrocketing emotions surging through their bodies.

He drew back gently. Then he got to his feet and walked to the door. Penelope struggled up on one elbow and looked at him in a dazed way. She could see him perfectly, for he was just the right distance away.

She could clearly see that tall, athletic figure, the strong legs, the crisp curls of his black hair, and that firm mouth which so recently had been pressed against her own.

He ran a hand through his hair. "Miss Mortimer," he said, "pray accept my deepest apologies," and he walked from the room.

Penelope turned her face into the pillow. But this time, she began to cry.

"My lord," said Pomfret, fussing about his master, "our cravat will not do!"

"What's up with the damned thing?"

"It is the soiled one we just removed."

"Oh, give me a clean one, and stop saying we, we, we the whole time. It drives me mad!"

"Yes, my lord," said Pomfret, although his eyes gleamed with pleasure. The cracks in the facade of The Perfect Gentleman were growing wider.

"And stop humming under your breath."

"Yes, my lord," said Pomfret cheerfully.

It was a subdued dinner. Penelope picked at her food, Lord Andrew maintained a brooding silence, the duchess was wondering how to get her revenge on Mr. Barcourt, and the duke was reading a magazine.

Penelope was wearing an opera gown of soft pale green muslin. It had a square neckline and puffed sleeves, the high-waisted fashion being simply cut and the gown ending in several flounces at the hem. All very modest on the face of it. But, Lord Andrew reflected, even had he not been told, he would have recognized the hand of a French designer. The muslin was cunningly cut and draped across the front to emphasize the swell of a young bosom, and the filmy cloth clung to the line of her hips. She was wearing one of the duchess's tiaras, a delicate thing of amethysts, tiny emeralds, and silver. About her white neck was a thin chain of emeralds and amethysts, the jewels burning brightly as if fueled by the youth and beauty of the skin against which they lay.

She had rolled back her long gloves to eat, and her small hands were red, with short, square nails. He was obscurely pleased at the mess of her hands and tried to concentrate his attention on them while he wondered what had made him kiss her. He had never behaved so badly before.

He glanced at her face. Her lashes were lowered over her eyes, those ridiculously long black lashes. His gaze returned to her hands. She dropped her fork with a clatter and blushed.

He knew his steady gaze was embarrassing her. He glared at his mother instead and was told testily to eat his food and stop gawping.

The duke was to accompany them to the opera, which meant a closed carriage, the duke considering travel in open carriages being responsible for all the ills in London. The duke sat facing the duchess, and Lord Andrew, beside his father, sat facing Penelope.

The carriage was old and the springs needed repair. As they lurched over the cobbles, Lord Andrew's knees were suddenly pressed against Penelope's. He felt as if an electric current from one of the new galvanizing machines had been shot through his body. He swung his knees sideways and looked unseeingly out of the window.

He had a longing for the undemanding company of his fiancée. He had been celibate for too long, he thought cynically. The best thing he could do would be to persuade Ann Worthy into an early marriage.

The Worthy family had been considering the same thing, but not because of any of the lusts of the flesh.

Miss Worthy's description of their drive had alarmed Mr. and Mrs. Worthy, for although their daughter only described how awful and peasantish the behavior of Penelope Mortimer had been, her parents, remembering only Penelope's dazzling beauty, were becoming worried at the thought of Lord Andrew being under the same roof as such a charmer. Miss Worthy had failed to tell them it had been the duchess's idea that Penelope accompany them on the drive, and so they understood Lord Andrew to have been the one who suggested that she join them.

Then late that afternoon, just before dinner, Mr. Benjamin Jepps, Miss Worthy's rejected suitor, had called and demanded a few private moments with Ann Worthy.

It is a reassuring fact that in this world there

is always someone for everyone, and Mr. Jepps was still very much in love with Miss Worthy.

He was a thin, clever gentleman of middle height, plainly and soberly dressed. He had large liquid brown eyes, a sharp nose, and a small fastidious mouth. His brown hair was a trifle thin, and he stiffened and thickened it with a mixture of sugar and water. He thought Miss Worthy supremely stupid and rejoiced in her vanities and her occasional lapses into the worst of fashion. He was one of those men who could not have tolerated a woman of any intelligence whatsoever, feeling he himself had enough at least for two. He adored red hair, and Miss Worthy was blessed with a large quantity of it.

While he felicitated her on her marriage, his agile brain was working out ways to put an end to her engagement. He regretted that his prosperous manufactories in the north, and the source of his wealth — although he kept that source well hidden — should have necessitated him being away for so long.

Miss Worthy, who was still smarting over that mysterious shared laughter between Lord Andrew and Penelope, found Mr. Jepps's continued admiration of her all that it should be. She even found herself regretting that he did not have a title. She added to her parents' worries by inviting Mr. Jepps to share their box at the opera.

Mr. Jepps rushed home to change into his evening clothes, anxious to meet Lord Andrew and to find out how best to confound this enemy.

So while the Worthy family watched the opera, Gluck's *Orpheus and Eurydice*, he raised his opera glasses and studied the Duke of Parkworth's box. His eyes lighted with glee on the dazzling vision that was Penelope Mortimer. He leaned toward Miss Worthy and whispered, "Who is that young lady with Lord Andrew?"

"A nobody," said Miss Worthy curtly. "Some undistinguished, impoverished miss from the country the duchess has seen fit to bring out."

"She resides, then, with the family?"

"Yes."

Mr. Jepps continued his study.

Lord Andrew had leaned his dark head close to Penelope's fair one. He was actually asking her about the costumes on the stage, and Penelope's replies were showing him that she could see very well. There was something in the way Lord Andrew's body leaned toward this Miss Mortimer and the way Miss Mortimer's cheeks had a becoming flush that spoke volumes to Mr. Jepps. With a satisfied little sigh, he put down his opera glasses and began to plot.

Lord Andrew was looking forward to a quiet tête-à-tête with his fiancée at the supper which was held afterwards before the opera ball. Miss Worthy was wearing an opera gown of old gold silk, which became her well. She was wearing a tiara of old gold and garnets, which was attractively set on the thick red tresses of her hair. Semiprecious stones were all the rage. No one who was anyone appeared in diamonds.

But somehow it appeared Mr. Jepps had managed to maneuver everyone into the one party at supper — himself and the Worthys, and Penelope and the duke and duchess and Lord Andrew.

Mr. Jepps sat himself next to Penelope and set himself to please. He discovered she liked novels and immediately assumed her taste ran to Gothic romances.

"There is a vastly interesting pile on the borders of Hertfordshire," said Mr. Jepps, gazing into Penelope's eyes while signaling to a footman to replenish their glasses. Mr. Jepps knew that a well-lubricated Ann Worthy could always be manipulated, and although he was giving Penelope all his attention, he wanted to make sure his beloved was kept in a malleable mood.

"Indeed," said Penelope politely.

"It is Dalby Castle, former seat of the Earls of Dalby. It is said to be haunted."

"By the ghost of a young maiden, no doubt," said Penelope.

Mr. Jepps gave her a sharp look, but her blue eyes were vague. "Yes," he said. "By the ghost of Lady Emmeline, the third earl's daughter. It is a most romantic place. I have been thinking for some time of organizing an outing. Would you care to go, Miss Mortimer?"

"Yes, she would," said the duchess, who had been studying Mr. Jepps as he talked to Penelope, and thinking, Twenty thousand a year at least. More perhaps. Unmarried. Couldn't be more suitable.

"And to complete the party," said Mr. Jepps, "Miss Worthy and Lord Andrew!"

Piqued at Mr. Jepps's interest in Penelope, Miss Worthy said, "Yes, I should like that above all things." No one waited for Lord Andrew's approval.

"Splendid. Then if the weather holds fine, we could set out the day after tomorrow at seven in the morning."

Mrs. Blenkinsop and Miss Amy Tilney came up at that point, followed by Lord Andrew's friend, Mr. Ian Macdonald. Lord Andrew did not want to find himself in the undiluted company of his fiancée, her rejected lover, and the increasingly disturbing Miss Mortimer. He hailed the newcomers with relief. "We are just planning an outing to Dalby Castle in Herts," he said. "I am sure Miss Tilney would like to join us, and you too, Ian."

Ian Macdonald read an odd look of appeal in his friend's eyes and said heartily he would be honored to be of the party. Maria Blenkinsop, seeing the look of fury on the duchess's face engendered by Miss Tilney being included in the invitation, accepted on behalf of her charge, adding maliciously, "I am sure, dear duchess, that we will both be glad of a break from the fatigues of chaperonage. Neither of us is young enough to face such a long outing with equanimity."

And so it was all set, and the rest of the evening passed pleasantly enough on the surface. Lord Andrew did not ask Penelope to dance, but Mr.

Jepps asked her twice and had the satisfaction of seeing his interest in the girl was causing Miss Worthy a certain amount of jealousy.

On the road home, the duchess lectured Penelope roundly on the merits of Mr. Jepps and ordered her to do her best to ensnare him. "Although," she added, "I must send for Mr. Barcourt tomorrow and ask him to explain himself."

"That will not be possible," said Lord Andrew, stretching his long legs in the carriage and then recoiling as from a snake when they brushed against Penelope's legs. "It was all the talk tonight. I wonder you did not hear it. Barcourt is claiming total loss of memory and has gone to the country until his brain has recovered."

"Pah!" said the duchess crossly. "Pah! Pooh!" And she was still pahing and poohing as they made their separate ways to bed.

Lord Andrew found himself praying for rain, but the day of Mr. Jepps's outing dawned fresh and fair. There was an hour's wait for Miss Worthy to put in an appearance, but Mr. Jepps had allowed for that, stating the time of departure as seven, but knowing they would be lucky if they got on the road by eight.

Lord Andrew led the way in his phaeton with Miss Worthy beside him, Mr. Jepps followed with Penelope, and Mr. Macdonald and Miss Tilney brought up the rear.

At one point on the journey, Penelope dropped her fan on the floor of the carriage. She leaned forward and groped about for it. Mr. Jepps bunched the reins in one hand and picked it up for her with the other. He wondered if she was very longsighted and, if so, if that defect could be put to some use. His sharp eyes had already noticed the way Lord Andrew's eyes had kept studiously avoiding Penelope before they set out. And Penelope *was* worth looking at. Although Mr. Jepps's goal was Ann Worthy, he did admit to himself it was pleasurable to be sitting beside such a fair partner. Penelope was wearing a thin gown of transparent blue muslin over an under-dress of blue silk. She wore a warm Paisley shawl about her shoulders, and her dashing little straw bonnet with a narrow brim was ideal for carriage wear as it did not flap about in the wind.

Mr. Jepps fell to questioning her about the duke's household and kept bringing up Lord Andrew's name and noticed that whenever he did so, Penelope became reserved.

The little party stopped at an inn for luncheon at eleven. Ian Macdonald was in high spirits and inclined to tease little Amy Tilney, who kept blushing with delight.

Mr. Jepps somehow had managed to sit beside Miss Worthy and keep her attention on himself. Lord Andrew asked Miss Worthy whether she would like to take a stroll with him in the inn garden, but she did not appear to hear. Quite out of charity with her, he forgot all his resolutions and, seeing that Penelope was already heading in the direction of the garden, followed her.

"What a lovely place," said Penelope, walking across the grass as he fell into step beside her. "Mr. Jepps appears to be a good organizer."

"Yes," said Lord Andrew curtly.

His feelings were mixed as he looked down at her. On the one hand, he was relieved she showed no sign of remembering that kiss. On the other, he had an obscure wish that she might somehow betray that the effect of it had startled her as much as it had him.

"Miss Worthy and Mr. Jepps appeared to be old friends," said Penelope.

"Yes, I believe their friendship to be of some years' standing."

"One never quite sees the attractions of one's own sex," ruminated Penelope. "Now, to quite a number of women, Miss Worthy would not appear as a heartbreaker."

"I do not discuss my fiancée with anyone," said Lord Andrew in chilly accents.

"Then we shall discuss Miss Tilney. Your mother regards her as an antidote, and she is possibly trying her best to view her from a male point of view. Matchmakers always think they know what the gentlemen like. But Miss Tilney appears to me to have great charm."

"She has a neat figure, is well mannered, and would do or say nothing to put any gentleman to the blush," said Lord Andrew.

"Unlike me?"

"Unlike you, Miss Mortimer."

"Then perhaps she and Mr. Macdonald are

well suited while you and I, my lord, are two of a kind."

"What can you mean?"

"Well, I may walk into lions' dens, but you, my lord, are engaged to one lady and yet bestow your kisses on another."

"If you were a lady," he said savagely, "you would forget that incident completely."

Penelope laughed. "Was it so very unpleasant?"

He turned on his heel and marched back into the inn and demanded to know if they were all going to hang around this cursed hostelry all day.

# Chapter Six

Mr. Jepps pointed out that as the castle was quite near, it would be easier if they all traveled in his barouche. So forceful and energetic were his arguments that the rest found themselves agreeing, although as they all crammed in beside Mr. Jepps, they began to wonder why they had so readily agreed, particularly Lord Andrew, who was jammed against the delectable side of Miss Penelope Mortimer and suffering from various uncomfortable physical reactions which he had hitherto believed only courtesans were supposed to prompt in gentlemen.

The day had turned very warm and sultry, more like high summer than an English spring day. The young leaves hung motionless on the trees, and spring flowers in the cottage gardens stood to attention like serried ranks of gaudy guardsmen.

The remains of Dalby Castle soon rose into view above the trees. It had been destroyed by the Parliamentarians in the Civil War, and only the Dungeon Tower remained standing. The Dalbys were proud of their ruin, and the grass around the tower had been cropped close by sheep to a billiard-table smoothness and swans swam among the water lilies on the moat which surrounded the tower and the piles of fallen masonry which were all that remained of the rest of the castle.

The small party alighted, and Penelope immediately went to look at the moat. Mr. Jepps raced after her and caught her just as she was about to step over the edge. He pulled her back and noticed the long-sighted way she blinked in the sunlight.

The half-formed plan that had been burgeoning in Mr. Jepp's agile brain sprang into flower. He knew the ruin well and knew there was a dark cellarlike chamber in the basement of the ruin which had a lock on the door as gardening tools and other estate equipment were stored there.

For the moment, he decided, it suited his interests to pay court to Miss Mortimer.

Miss Worthy looked decidedly peeved. She had not made much effort to engage the interest of her fiancé on the outing because he had already been snared, so to speak. But she had expected Mr. Jepps to remain her devoted admirer.

Lord Andrew had made up his mind to devote the day to his fiancée and put Penelope out of his mind. The normally shy and diffident Miss Tilney was delighted with the easygoing, undemanding company of Ian Macdonald.

Seeing that everyone else was occupied in strolling around the edge of the moat, Mr. Jepps said to Penelope, "Come with me and I will show you the most dark and romantic room at the bottom of the tower."

"I do not find dark rooms very romantic," said

the ever- practical Penelope. But at that moment, Miss Worthy, walking in the distance with Lord Andrew, stumbled, and he put an arm around her waist to support her.

Penelope felt a sharp pain somewhere about the region of her heart. The idea of getting away from the very sight of Lord Andrew became welcoming, so she added, "But if you care to show it to me, I shall be glad to go."

They walked sedately together out of the sunlight into the shadow of the tower. Mr. Jepps led the way inside and then down a crumbling flight of stairs to a stout door in the basement.

"And shall we find terrible instruments of torture?" asked Penelope sarcastically.

"Undoubtedly. I am anxious to see the room myself, for I have never been here before," lied Mr. Jepps. He turned the key in the lock and stood aside to let Penelope past. She walked into the cold, dark chamber lit faintly by light from a barred window well above her head. She looked about her blindly. "What is here, Mr. Jepps? It is so very dark. No rack or thumbscrew?"

"Excuse me!" called Mr. Jepps. "Forgot something. Back in a trice." He slammed the door.

Why leave me here? thought Penelope, half-amused, half-exasperated. And why is it that the gentlemen always believe we females will fall into Gothic raptures at the very sight of a dirty old room? From the sound of lapping water, she gathered the room was under the level of the moat outside.

She put on her glasses and looked about her. There were piles of gardening implements and empty sacks.

After some minutes, she began to feel cold and went to the door and turned the handle, only to find it firmly locked.

"Silly man!" she said to herself. "Oh, well, he will be back soon enough." She stowed her spectacles safely away and began to walk up and down the room.

Mr. Jepps hurried across the turf to where Lord Andrew was walking with Miss Worthy. He could see from the expressions on their faces that they had been having a row, which in fact they had. Miss Worthy had called Penelope a bold minx and had said she was flirting shamelessly with poor Mr. Jepps, and Lord Andrew had remarked acidly that she, Miss Worthy, was the one who had been flirting shamelessly. So when Mr. Jepps asked for a word in private with Lord Andrew, Miss Worthy turned sulkily away.

"What is it?" asked Lord Andrew testily.

"It is Miss Mortimer. She is desirous to speak to you."

"I cannot think why. Where is she?"

"In a room in the basement of the tower."

Lord Andrew gave a click of exasperation. He was beginning to dislike Mr. Jepps. He thought him a poor, fussy sort of fellow.

"Very well. Lead the way."

Mr. Jepps ushered Lord Andrew down the stairs to the underground chamber. He unlocked the door, ignoring Lord Andrew's startled question as to why Miss Mortimer was locked in. Penelope swung round. "Thank goodness you are come," she said. "You locked me in, Mr. Jepps!"

"What is it you want to see me about?" asked Lord Andrew, striding forward. Mr. Jepps retreated swiftly and slammed and locked the door again. Ignoring the furious cries coming faintly from inside, he made his way upstairs and out into the warmth of the sunlight.

Now his biggest task lay ahead. He had to persuade the others to return to London, to persuade them that Lord Andrew and Penelope had already left. Clouds were rising up in the sky, and a blustery wind had rushed out of nowhere, hissing in the trees and ruffling the waters of the moat.

He was sure Ann Worthy, activated by jealousy, would readily believe him, but Ian Macdonald and Miss Tilney were going to be difficult.

He cocked his head to one side, but no shout or scream escaped from the thick walls of the underground room. If they could climb up to that barred window, they might make themselves heard. Better to move quickly.

He went straight to Ann Worthy.

"A most odd thing has happened," he cried. "Lord Andrew and Miss Mortimer have gone off — walked off — declaring their intention of going to the inn. I think it very strange behavior in a man who is affianced to you, Miss Worthy. Very odd, and so I told him. He told me to mind my own business, and Miss Mortimer giggled. If we leave now, we can catch them up on the road, and you may demand an explanation."

"And he shall give me one!" said Miss Worthy, quite beside herself with fury.

Ian Macdonald had already taken a strong dislike to Miss Worthy. He was also accustomed to his friend, The Perfect Gentleman, never putting a foot wrong. So if Lord Andrew had decided to walk back to the inn with Miss Mortimer, it followed he probably had some highly conventional and boring reason for doing so.

Mr. Jepps heaved a sigh of relief. It was all so much easier than he had imagined. He would send a messenger from London the following morning to let the couple out. By that time they would have spent the night together, and Lord Andrew would be obliged to marry Miss Mortimer. Mr. Jepps was sure that Lord Andrew would challenge him to a duel. But he was not afraid of that. He would accept the challenge and, since dueling was illegal, alert the authorities to arrest Lord Andrew.

Now one more obstacle lay ahead. Lord Andrew's phaeton.

As soon as they reached the inn, Mr. Jepps urged the party to go inside. Then he ran round to the stables. He was in luck. An unsavory-looking idler, the type who hangs around horse fairs, was leaning against a post, chewing a straw. In a hurried whisper, he agreed to pay the man ten pounds to drive Lord Andrew's horses and phaeton to London and leave them in the Park Street mews. The fellow was paid five pounds in advance and was to call at Mr. Jepps's London address that evening for the other half.

Then Mr. Jepps strolled back into the inn. Miss Worthy was wondering aloud why they had not overtaken the couple on the road. Mr. Jepps went off to see the landlord and explained that Miss Worthy's fiancé had taken off with another lady. It would take time to break the news. The landlord was to wait an hour and then enter the coffee room and say someone had seen the couple driving off. As a matter of fact, Mr. Jepps said, handing over some guineas to the gratified landlord and drooping one eyelid in a vulgar wink, the couple were putting up with an accommodating friend in the vicinity and had sent their carriage back to London to throw dust in the eyes of the party. Flattered to be included in all this aristocratic intrigue, the landlord agreed to play his part.

Mr. Jepps had no fear of the repercussions that would arise from his machinations. He was a very wealthy man and was confident of bribing his way out of any situation. He might even have to travel abroad for a time but, without Lord Andrew, he was confident that Miss Worthy would wait for him. In fact, flight, rather than waiting around to be challenged to a duel, might be the wisest course.

Ian Macdonald began to assume long before the landlord put in an appearance that his friend, Lord Andrew, had finally come to his senses and decided to do something wrong for once in his life — namely, ditching a sour-faced fiancée for that blond charmer. He decided to play along, only remarking that the weather had changed and they had better set out before the rain came. But Miss Worthy hung on until the landlord finally removed any hope from her angry breast. She drove back to London with Mr. Jepps, breathing fire and vengeance and breaches of promise. Mr. Jepps listened sympathetically to this tirade and insisted on entering her house so he could support her as she told her parents of Lord Andrew's perfidy.

Mr. and Mrs. Worthy listened in horror. There was only one thing to be done. They called for their carriage and set out for Park Street to complain to the duchess about her son's behavior.

The duchess laughed at them. Lord Andrew had never behaved badly in his life, she said, and was not likely to start now. There would be some very conventional explanation. Much reassured, the Worthys left, not knowing that as soon as they were out of the ducal town house, the duchess went into a fit of hysterics, threatening to string Penelope Mortimer up by the thumbs should she ever see her again.

Meanwhile, in the underground chamber, Penelope Mortimer was standing on top of Lord Andrew's shoulders sawing desperately at the bars at the window with a saw they had found buried under the pile of gardening tools. "Cannot you try a little harder?" he called up.

"I am trying as hard as I can," said Penelope crossly. "You do it if you think you can do any better."

"Don't be silly. How can *I* stand on *your* shoulders? Keep sawing."

"I've done two bars already," sighed Penelope, squinting at the window. "It looks very dark outside."

"I do not care if there is a blizzard raging. That cur Jepps planned to make us spend the night together so that he could marry Miss Worthy. What a flat I was to be so taken in! But we must get out of here. I'm damned if I'll be made to marry you."

"Who would want to marry *you*, of all people?" said Penelope furiously.

"Shut up. Keep sawing and just shut up."

Penelope sawed and sawed. The bars were old and rusty, but she was exhausted when the last bar broke and fell into the moat.

"Don't come down," said Lord Andrew. "Do you know how to swim?"

"Yes."

"Then jump through the window and swim across the moat."

"Have you no feeling, sir? I shall be soaked to the skin. Furthermore, it has started to rain."

"If you do not go through that window of your own accord, then I shall throw you through," said Lord Andrew. "Get a move on; there's a good girl. My shoulders are aching, and you are not making things easier by jumping about on them and putting up missish arguments."

Penelope threw the white blur of his face a baleful look. She hauled herself up by the remaining stumps of the sawn bars, tore her gown dragging her body across them, and tumbled headlong into the moat. Something heavy underwater brushed against her body. Penelope immediately thought of large carp with large teeth and frantically swam to the surface and struck out for where she believed the far side of the moat to be.

"I declare you are as blind as a bat," said Lord Andrew's voice from somewhere above her head. "The other way, girl."

Penelope turned around and struck out away from the tower again and this time reached the opposite side of the moat. She clambered out, long trails of green, slimy weed hanging from her torn and soaking dress. Clouds were boiling black in the sky above, and cold, driving rain pounded down on her head. Her frivolous little bonnet floated on the surface of the moat.

The great wave resulting from Lord Andrew diving into the moat from the window submerged the bonnet, which disappeared completely from view. Penelope began to cry. All at once it seemed the most tragic thing in the world to lose that pretty bonnet.

Had the circumstances been more civilized,

then Lord Andrew would have soothed Penelope and dried her tears. But the increasing storm raging above made him behave as if he were still in the army.

"Why are you crying?" he demanded harshly.

"I've lost my bonnet. You drowned it," said Penelope pathetically.

"Of all the idiotish girls. Pull yourself together this instant, Miss Mortimer!"

Penelope gave a defiant sob and looked down at the ruin of her dress. "There is not much left *to* pull together. It is so dark. What time is it?"

He pulled out his watch and looked at it. "I suppose it must have stopped when I hit the water. It is about nine in the evening."

"Nine!"

"It is all your fault, you know. You took hours sawing those bars."

"It may amaze you to know that bar sawing is not a ladylike accomplishment. But who knows? They may even begin to teach it in the seminaries and dame schools along with the art of lock picking."

"Come along. I do not suppose it is of any use looking for my carriage. I am sure Jepps found a way to get rid of it. What I fail to understand is why Ian Macdonald did not stay around to find us. Well, it is of no use standing here wondering. We must find shelter."

Had Lord Andrew turned right on the road outside the ruined castle instead of to the left, they would have found themselves back in the village where he had left his carriage, the landlord would have recognized them, and they would have been made welcome. But the blackness of the night as they scurried along under the trees was bewildering. They half ran, half stumbled along the road under the increasing ferocity of the storm.

They had been hurrying along like this for over an hour when the flickering lights of a village appeared out of the blackness.

At the edge of the village was a small inn called The Green Man, its sign swinging in the wind.

Lord Andrew strode up to the inn with Penelope tottering behind him, and pushed open the door.

He found himself in a small hall. He rang a brass bell on a side table. Penelope came in and stood, shivering.

"Shut the door behind you," snapped Lord Andrew. "Or are you not cold enough?"

A small, stocky landlord appeared from the tap and eyed the bedraggled couple warily.

"And what would you two be wanting?" he asked.

"I am Lord Andrew Childe," said Lord Andrew haughtily, "and, as you can see, we have been caught in the storm. We wish rooms where we can dry ourselves, and we need dinner, for I am sharp-set."

"It's a fine lord you make," said the landlord. "Where is your carriage? Your servants?"

"I went for an outing and was tricked. I do

not know where my carriage is." Penelope gave a dismal sneeze.

The landlord's wife came out to join him, demanding to know what was up.

"This here gent," said the landlord, his voice laden with sarcasm, "says as how he's a lord and he's asking for rooms and dinner."

"This is a respectable inn. . . ." began the landlady. Penelope coughed and sneezed and shivered. The landlord's wife looked at her, and her face softened. "But the poor lady is mortal wet. We have only one room, and you're welcome to that if you pay your shot in advance. But only if you are married, mind."

Lord Andrew suddenly caught a glimpse of himself in an old, greenish mirror over the hall table. His black hair was plastered down on his forehead, his cravat to his coat. He looked at Penelope. She had not only lost her bonnet in the moat, but her shawl as well. Her filmy muslin gown clung to her shivering body.

"Yes, we are married," he said. He fished in the pocket in his tails, relieved to find a rouleau of guineas still there. He pulled it out and began to shake gold coins out into his hand. "How much?" he asked curtly. "We will need to hire a carriage after we have dined."

The landlord's jaw dropped when he saw the gold. "I don't know as there's a spare gig around here at this time of night, my lord. Why don't you and your lady go upstairs, and we'll call you when dinner is ready. There's a couple o' gents in the private parlor, but they're nigh finished."

"Good," said Lord Andrew. "How much?"

But the sight of that gold had worked wonders on the landlord. "You may pay your shot when you leave, my lord," he said, bowing low. "I am Mr. Carter, and this is my wife, Abigail. Mrs. Carter, do take my lord and my lady to their room."

"But I'm not —" Penelope began weakly, and then let out a scream as Lord Andrew stamped on her foot.

"I am so sorry, my love," said Lord Andrew, taking her arm in a firm grip. "An accident. Come along. You are in no fit state to talk," he added in a threatening tone of voice. "Mrs. Carter, we would be obliged if you could find us dressing gowns of some sort. We cannot dine in our wet clothes, and I fear we have no others."

"I'm sure I can find you something," said Mrs. Carter, made as cheerful and obsequious as her husband by the sight of that gold.

They followed the landlord's wife up a crooked staircase and along a short corridor. "It's our best bedroom," said Mrs. Carter proudly.

Lord Andrew and Penelope stood shivering while Mr. Carter and a waiter entered with a coal and logs and proceeded to build up a roaring fire. Mrs. Carter disappeared only to reappear shortly with flannel nightgowns and two dressing gowns, both men's and both made of coarse wool, and two red Kilmarnock nightcaps.

A maidservant came in with cans of hot water

and rough huckaback towels. The landlord then delivered a tray with a bottle of white brandy and two glasses and a kettle of boiling water.

"We will leave you to change, my lord. My wife will take your wet clothes down to the kitchen to be cleaned and dried. The private parlor is next door to your room, so you may dine in your night rail without disturbing any of the other guests."

Lord Andrew wanted to say that they planned to set out for London as soon as their clothes were dried, but Penelope looked white and exhausted, and he felt he would tackle further explanations when they had dined.

Finally Penelope and Lord Andrew were left alone.

"If you will go out into the corridor, my lord," said Penelope weakly, "I will change my clothes."

"There is no need for that," he said. "I will draw the bed hangings to form a screen. You undress on this side in front of the fire, and I will change on the other. First, have something to drink."

"Later," said Penelope.

"No, now!"

He poured her a stiff glass of brandy and topped it up with hot water and stood over her until she had drunk it.

Then he picked up his nightclothes and went to the other side of the bed, drawing the chintz hangings closed to form a screen.

Penelope looked dizzily about her. The room

had an odd way of moving up and down. It was like being on board ship, or rather, like the descriptions she had read about life on a sailing ship. She removed her thin, sopping clothes, those summer clothes which had been so beautiful earlier that day, and pulled on the nightgown, and then wrapped the man's dressing gown tightly around her. She was leaning over the fire, trying to dry her hair, when Lord Andrew came round to join her. He seized a towel and rubbed her hair with it and then opened her reticule to look for a comb.

"No," screamed Penelope, snatching the reticule from him. Ill and faint as she felt, she still did not want him to see those glasses.

She took out a tortoiseshell comb, drew the strings of her reticule tight, and then tried to comb her hair, but the comb kept getting caught in the tangles.

"Here, let me," said Lord Andrew. He tilted up her face and gently eased the comb through the tangled mess of her drying hair.

"Why did you say we were man and wife?" asked Penelope. "Are you trying to compromise me?"

"I am trying to stop us from both getting the ague," he said impatiently. "We could not possibly have gone further in our soaking state. We will set out for London as soon as possible."

A buffet of wind hurled rain against the windows. "I am so tired," said Penelope wretchedly.

"You will feel better when you have dined,"

he said. He looked at the pathetic little figure in front of him with a sharp stab of concern. Anger at the way he had been so easily tricked combined with the rigors of running through the storm to shelter had made him treat Penelope very badly indeed. He had always believed women to be delicate and frail creatures. What if she fell ill? He would never forgive himself. Why hadn't he left her in the shelter of that tower room and gone for help himself? She must be exhausted after sawing those bars. But he could not have done it himself. There had been nothing to stand on, and it had been difficult enough for him to clamber up the wall and out of that window.

The landlord appeared to announce dinner — "though it be more of a supper," he explained, "dinner being at four."

Penelope and Lord Andrew went through to the private parlor. Dinner consisted of salt fish, leg of mutton boiled with capers, roasted loin of beef, and plum and plain puddings. The landlord explained a wedding was to be held at the inn the next day, and the food was part of the preparations for it. Any other time, and my lord would have had to be content with a cold collation.

After they had finished eating in silence and the cover had been withdrawn and the port and fruit and nuts set on the plain wood, the couple found themselves alone.

"Now, what am I to do with that fellow Jepps?" said Lord Andrew, half to himself. "If I challenge him to a duel, then ten to one he will accept but then alert the authorities. I think I will content myself with smashing his face in."

"He wants Miss Worthy," said Penelope sleepily. "He is very much in love."

"Nonsense."

"Why nonsense? He has gone to great lengths to prevent your marriage. He must know you could kill him, although you do not look very ferocious in that funny dressing gown and with that red nightcap on your head."

"You look pretty silly yourself," said Lord Andrew, although he privately thought she looked very endearing in the enormous dressing gown and with her silvery-fair hair drying in a cloud about her head.

"The thing is this," went on Lord Andrew, pouring a glass of port for Penelope and then one for himself. "We will now see if our clothes are dry enough and borrow a greatcoat for you to wear and then see if we can hire a gig. We shall set out for London. We shall say we escaped from the tower, hired a gig, and journeyed through the night. The fact that we were masquerading at this inn as man and wife, if only for dinner, must never come out. Do you understand?"

"Yes, my lord," yawned Penelope.

"You had better wear my ring until we are clear of this inn." He drew a heavy gold and sapphire ring from his finger and handed it over. Penelope slid it over her fourth finger. "It's too big," she said. "It wobbles."

"Then crook your finger round it. Now, go and lie down for half an hour while I make the arrangements."

When Penelope had left, he summoned the landlord and ordered him to find some sort of carriage and horses.

The landlord scratched his head in perplexity. "I don't know if I can do that at this time of night," he said. "My own gig's broke. Mayhap squire would have something, but he's an old man, and it won't do to rouse him this time of the night. Then there's Mr. Baxter over at Five Elms —"

"Do your best," said Lord Andrew. "But we must leave for London this night."

Mrs. Carter brought their clothes up from the kitchen. The mud had been sponged from them, but they were still damp. Lord Andrew spread them over two chairs in front of the bedroom fire to dry.

Then he walked over to the bed and looked down at Penelope. She was fast asleep, one small red hand bunched into a fist to hold his ring safe.

What a brute I am, he thought with remorse. If only I could allow this child to sleep. Mercy, but I am exhausted myself. Perhaps just half an hour . . .

He stretched out beside her. She moved in her sleep and, with an incoherent little murmur, snuggled against him.

He was filled with a great wave of tenderness. He put his arms about her and held her close and rested his chin on the top of her head. The bedroom was warm and comfortable. The sensations coursing through his body were languorous and sweet.

He kissed her hair and his heavy eyelids began to droop. It would do no harm to kiss her goodnight. He moved his lips to her sleeping mouth and kissed her gently.

His head slid down to rest on her bosom, and with his arms still tightly about her, he fell asleep.

"Morning, my lord!"

Penelope and Lord Andrew slowly came awake. Sunlight was pouring into the room. Mrs. Carter was standing smiling down at them indulgently. Lord Andrew realized his arms were still about Penelope, and his legs appeared to have become tangled up with hers during the night. They were both still lying on top of the bedclothes.

"Why did you not call me when the carriage was ready?" he said, sitting up.

"To be sure, there was nothing we could do about getting you anything in the middle of such a storm," said Mrs. Carter. "Mr. Carter, he came up after supper to tell you so, but you was sleeping like babies, and so he left you. 'Tis six in the morning. Mr. Carter says I was to wake you as soon as we got a gig, which we did, and it's the smartest little turnout you ever did see. Mr. Baxter himself brought it over and is waiting to see your lordship."

"Thank you," said Lord Andrew, while his mind raced. Provided Penelope held her tongue, they could still be in London before anyone was awake — the fashionable world not stirring until two in the afternoon. He dismissed Mrs. Carter and stripped off his dressing gown and nightgown and began to wash himself. The angry jerk of the bed curtains as the startled Penelope shut off the interesting view of his naked body sounded behind him. He felt himself blush as he had not blushed since he was an adolescent. How could he, who had been so perfect until so recently, have forgotten the simple proprieties?

After a rushed breakfast, they were both at last seated in a small gig pulled by a glossy little pony. Mr. Baxter had supplied them with greatcoats, for although the sun was shining once more, the morning was chilly.

Lord Andrew wondered whether to take this country gentleman into his confidence and then decided against it. The explanations would prove too embarrassing. He thanked Mr. Baxter again, grimly introduced Penelope as his wife, and promised to send his servant back with the gig and pony the following day.

Penelope was glad of the greatcoat. Her gown had shrunk and was stretched indecently over her body. Lord Andrew, too, was glad of his covering. His clothes, although they had not shrunk, were wrinkled and shabby-looking. After various efforts with the mangled remains of his cravat, he had decided to wear his cambric shirt open at the neck.

He thought gloomily that he and Penelope looked like a couple of gypsies and could only hope some parish constable would not stop them and accuse them of stealing the gig.

# Chapter Seven

A thin mist was rising from the fields as they journeyed along. Drifts of may blossom scented the sunny air. Busy birds hopped along the thickets, and smoke from cottage chimneys rose lazily into the air. Soon, apart from a few broken branches and twigs lying on the road, there was no sign of the terrible storm of the night before.

"I have never made so many mistakes in my life before," said Lord Andrew, breaking a silence that had lasted over an hour.

"Well, it was a bit silly, if you don't want to be compromised, to lie in bed hugging me," said Penelope practically.

"I was cold."

"Then next time put the blankets over you!"

"There won't be a next time."

"Oh, yes there will," said Penelope nastily. "Someone as easily gulled as you will no doubt end up in a brothel convinced he is staying at the most respectable posting house."

"I was wondering why I treated you with so little consideration yesterday," said Lord Andrew evenly, "but now I realize why. It is because you have no delicacy, no shame, no —"

"Shut up, do, you pompous ass!"

"How dare you speak to me thus, Miss Mortimer! How dare you!"

116

"That is exactly how you speak to me. It is amazing how people who are expert at dishing out the nastiest medicine do not know how to take it themselves."

Penelope, in her way, was as stubborn and arrogant as Lord Andrew. If one of them had said at that point, "I love you," then the row would have been at an end. But both were suffering badly from frustrated physical desire, neither would admit it to themselves, and so they traveled on, sniping at each other, each searching their tired brains for the most wounding things to say.

When the sun had risen high in the sky, Penelope had told Lord Andrew in a conversational tone of voice that he was, in fact, not at all handsome and lacked breeding and elegance, and Lord Andrew had told Miss Penelope Mortimer that there was something blowsy and peasantlike about her blond looks which must set up revulsion in the fastidious breast.

By the time the pair, made stiff and haughty by bad temper, sailed into a richly appointed posting house demanding refreshment, it came like a douche of cold water to both to find themselves turned off the premises with insults.

"*Well!*" said Penelope furiously as they climbed back into the gig. "What a dreadful man. He said you were a highwayman and I was your moll! He refused to serve us. He said we were dirty gallows birds! Why did you not thrash him for his insolence?"

117

"I took one look at you, my sweet, and saw the force of his argument."

"It was you he was addressing. And you do look remarkably slovenly."

The pony plodded on. Lord Andrew stared at its ears and wondered what it would be like to strangle Penelope Mortimer.

"I am very hungry," she said at last. "Are you going to find us some food or are you going to sulk all day?"

"I never sulk."

"Fiddle. You are in an arch sulk. Here is a village and there is a shop. Now, if we bought some bread and cheese and some wine, we could find a comfortable field and have a picnic."

He was about to tell her he now had no intention of stopping until they reached London, but he was very hungry and the pony needed a rest.

He reined in and, without a word, went off to buy various things, eventually coming back with them all packed up in a new wicker basket.

"Walk on," he said to the pony, and not looking at Penelope, he stared straight ahead.

"Truce," said Penelope in a small voice.

"What?"

"You heard. We can either decide to have a pleasurable picnic and make what we can of our journey or we can continue to be nasty to each other and get indigestion."

He began to laugh. For some reason, his bad temper evaporated like the morning mist. "Truce, Miss Mortimer," he cried, "and there is the place for our picnic." He pointed with his whip to a little stream which tumbled down through a wood of young oak and birch.

Soon the pony was unhitched and they were seated on a flat rock by the stream, drinking wine out of thick tumblers and eating ham and bread and cheese.

The sun glittered on the sapphire on Penelope's finger. She drew the ring off and handed it to him. "I unmarry you, Lord Andrew Childe," she said, "and with this ring I thee divorce."

He took it and tossed it up and down in his hand. Then he handed it back to her. "I want you to have it," he said.

"Why?"

"I think our adventures need a memento. When you are old and staid, you can look at it and say to your grandchildren, 'I remember the day I got locked in a castle dungeon with the terrible Lord Andrew.'"

"Then I shall keep it, but I shall remain a spinster, I assure you."

She had taken off her coat. Her gown was stretched across her figure. He lay on his back in the sun and half closed his eyes. Through his lashes he could see a strand of torn muslin on the front of her gown fluttering in the light breeze. It was as well the underdress had remained intact, he thought, although what she was wearing left little to the imagination.

"We must go soon," he said, but he did not

move. "Duty waits."

"Duty?"

"Duty to my parents, duty to Miss Worthy, duty to my name. I cannot marry you, Miss Mortimer."

"I do not expect you to. I look for the impossible anyway. I look for a man who would marry me for love."

He opened his eyes and rolled over on his side, propping his head on his hand to look up at her as she sat next to him.

"You will find such a one, Miss Mortimer," he said. "You are very lovable."

Penelope forced a laugh. "What! I? A blowsy peasant?"

"I did not mean a word of it. You are beautiful and courageous, and your hair is like the sun and your eyes like the blue sky."

"I liked you better when you cursed me," said Penelope. "You have no right to speak to me so. Let us leave."

He stood up and held down his hand and drew her to her feet. The river chuckled and bubbled, the pony lazily cropped the green grass, and the lightest of breezes rustled the leaves of the trees above and lifted the silken curls of her hair.

"Put on your coat," he said quietly.

"It is too hot."

"You are revealing too much."

"Oh!" Penelope blushed and stooped down to pick up her coat. He took it from her and held it out. She slipped her arms into the sleeves, her back to him. He drew her against him and they stood silent, listening to the river.

"Back to London," he said softly in her ear.

"Back to London," echoed Penelope on a sigh.

They collected the remains of their picnic and packed them in the basket, not looking at each other. They harnessed up the horse and climbed into the gig. The little pony gallantly plodded along the roads, which were now white with dust.

They did not speak again the whole journey home. As they trotted along Piccadilly to Park Street, Penelope could feel a dark weight pressing on her heart. There were explanations to be given, and then the life of the Season would go on. Lord Andrew would squire Miss Worthy to balls and parties, and she, Penelope Mortimer, would put up with a few more weeks of the Season before returning home. Penelope knew if she refused one more suitor, then the duchess would tire of her.

Lord Andrew and Penelope were told that the duchess was in the red saloon on the ground floor. The butler held open the door and announced them.

Penelope ducked just in time. A vase sailed over her head and smashed against the door jamb.

"Stop it immediately," said Lord Andrew, seizing his mother's arm as the duchess was about to follow the vase with a bowl of flowers.

"Scheming harlot!" raged the duchess. "Oh, God! Strike this poor wounded mother dead!

What have I done that I should be cursed with a fool for a son?" She ducked under Lord Andrew's arm and flew at Penelope. Penelope darted off with the duchess after her, finally shaking her off by running over the sofa. The duchess tripped and fell on her face on the floor, where she lay sobbing and screaming and drumming her fists. Lord Andrew jerked his mother upright and forced her down into the depths of an armchair while she continued to scream, not out of fury but because the pressure was forcing the bones of her stays to dig into her back.

At his wits' end, Lord Andrew seized the bowl of flowers his mother had been trying to throw at Penelope and upended the contents on the duchess's head.

There was a deathly silence. The duchess stared at her son while hothouse roses and dahlias hung dripping from her muslin cap.

"Now, listen," said Lord Andrew quietly. "I am still engaged to Miss Worthy. Nothing happened. Miss Mortimer and I were victims of a cruel practical joke. Do you understand?"

"But where *were* you? You *must* have spent the night together."

"We traveled all night and most of today. We borrowed a gig and a little pony which could not travel fast. Is that not so, Miss Mortimer?"

"Oh, yes," said Penelope.

"Why did you not say so in the first place?" said the duchess, glaring round the room. Three liveried footmen who had been pretending to be busy about their duties exited sideways with their traditional sliding step like so many gold and scarlet crabs. Perkins, the lady's maid, who had been crouched in the corner while the scene was at its height, rushed forward to fuss about her mistress.

"So," went on the duchess brightly, pushing Perkins away, "we must prepare for the evening. Penelope, my love, put on the silver ballgown, I beseech you. There is a turtle supper followed by a masked ball at the Foxtons'."

"Miss Mortimer is in no fit state to go anywhere," said Lord Andrew.

But Penelope, relieved the dreadful scene was over, said, "I am quite recovered," and slipped quietly from the room.

Lord Andrew stayed only to tell his mother the full story of Mr. Jepps's trickery before going off to change. Pomfret, his valet, took one ecstatic look at the wreck of The Perfect Gentleman and burst into tears of gratitude, much to Lord Andrew's extreme annoyance.

Once more groomed and elegant, he drove straight to Mr. Jepps's town house. He was not very surprised to learn that Mr. Jepps had left for an unknown destination. He went on to the Worthys' house.

Miss Worthy and her parents were just sitting down to dinner. Lord Andrew was asked to join them. He was relieved that no one seemed inclined to shout or rail at him. His vastly edited story of his adventures was heard in attentive silence. Miss Worthy's green eyes began to glow with pleasure. Lord Andrew's tired, bored voice made his adventures, and the company of Penelope Mortimer, appear gratifyingly dull. Added to that, Miss Worthy found it extremely flattering that dear Mr. Jepps should have gone to such lengths to try to break her engagement. Although she outwardly expressed horror at his behavior and said, yes, Mr. Jepps must be found and punished, in her heart she wished the absent Mr. Jepps well. It was a pity he did not have a title.

After sympathizing with Lord Andrew's hardships, Mr. Worthy said, "You will, alas, be too fatigued to accompany us to the Foxtons'. There is to be a turtle supper, which is why we are dining so frugally at the moment." Mr. Worthy waved a deprecating hand to apologize for the mere five courses which had been set before them.

Lord Andrew opened his mouth to say that yes, he was too tired to attend. Life felt very stale, flat, and dull. Life was perfect again. He was engaged to a suitable lady, and he must forget he ever lay beside a stream with Penelope Mortimer at his side. But Penelope would be there. She would be so very tired. She would need someone to look after her. He suddenly remembered reaching for her reticule to find her comb and how she had snatched it from him. What had she not wanted him to see? A letter from some country lover?

"The least I can do after my escapade is to escort my long-suffering fiancée," he said with a charming smile. "You must excuse me. I must return to find a mask. I have certain arrangements to make. I shall see you there."

When he reached Park Street, he made his way up to his room. He passed Penelope's bedroom door, then went back and pushed it open. Penelope was sitting in an armchair in front of the bedroom fire. She was dressed in a silver net ballgown. A delicate headdress of artificial flowers and silver wire was on her fashionably dressed head. She was fast asleep.

He saw the reticule she had carried on the adventures lying on a table beside the bed. He went over quietly, picked it up, and drew open the strings. It was empty.

He turned about and looked thoughtfully at the still-sleeping Penelope. There was a reticule at her feet, a frivolous little bag decorated with silver threadwork and pearls. He crossed the room and picked it up, and examined the contents. He slowly drew out an ugly pair of steel-framed spectacles.

He held them up to the light. The lenses were strongly magnified. "Longsighted," he murmured. "Poor little thing. Not much of a guilty secret." He put them back in the bag and quietly left the room.

He felt wretchedly tired during the turtle supper, and worse after the dancing had commenced. There were seemingly endless energetic country dances. The full force of what she now regarded as her tremendous attraction for the opposite sex had gone to Miss Worthy's head. Her eyes glittered with excitement through the slits of her mask. Not knowing her initial attraction for Lord Andrew — apart from her birth and bank balance — was that she was quiet and restful, she chattered and flirted every time the movement of the dance brought them together. It was a relief to escape from her but not very pleasurable to stand and watch Penelope besieged by admirers. He noticed with a sinking heart that the middle-aged Duke of Harford — one of the few gentlemen who was not wearing a mask — whose wife had died two years ago, was unable to take his eyes off Penelope. Now, if *he* proposed, Lord Andrew felt sure his mother would lock Penelope up and keep her on bread and water until she agreed to marry the duke.

He turned and went into the room set aside for refreshments. Ian Macdonald hailed him and demanded to know the full story.

Loyalty to his fiancée stopped Lord Andrew from telling the truth. In a flat voice, he recounted the same story he had told the Worthys, adding that Jepps had fled.

"Well, I am sorry for you," said Ian. "I had the most prodigious good time. Little Miss Tilney made sweet company."

"Do not mislead her, my friend," cautioned Lord Andrew. "She is young and no doubt does not know you are a hardened bachelor."

126

"I am not hardened in the least. I had not met any lady before who interested me enough."

"And Miss Tilney does?"

"Greatly. I only saw her yesterday, and I miss her dreadfully already." He looked through the door of the refreshment room, and his face lit up. "Why, there she is! And accompanied by her dragon."

Lord Andrew caught his friend's arm. "Stay a moment. Never say you mean to propose!"

"Not here and now," said Ian Macdonald. "I shall call on the Blenkinsop female tomorrow. What is it to you? You are going to be married yourself."

"Yes. Yes, of course." Lord Andrew released his arm and watched Ian Macdonald threading his way through the dancers to Miss Tilney's side. Miss Tilney was masked, and Lord Andrew would have been hard put to it to identify her. Love obviously sharpened the sight wonderfully. He would not have recognized Miss Worthy had she not accosted him first. If Ian proposed, he thought gloomily, then his mother would make sure Penelope became engaged to someone, any-one, as well. Where *was* Penelope? His eyes raked the ballroom. Now he knew how dreadfully long-sighted she was, he feared she had wandered off into the garden, where there was a small orna-mental pool.

He walked through the ballroom to the long windows overlooking the garden. One window was open onto a terrace. He walked out and stood with his hands on the balustrade, his eyes searching the garden.

Then he saw a glint of silver over in the far corner. He walked down the steps leading from the terrace and then round the little lake with its ornamental fountain and into the darkness of the shrubbery.

Penelope, wearing a silver mask to match her gown, sat on a marble bench under the drooping branches of a lilac tree. The sooty air was heavily scented with lilac blossom. She started in alarm as he came up to her, her eyes only seeing vaguely the black velvet of his mask.

He sat down beside her and said, "Do not be afraid."

"Oh, it's you," said Penelope in a flat voice.

"You do not know me, ma'am. I am a stranger to you."

Penelope let out a gurgle of laughter. "We can hardly be strangers. I think we must be two of the most exhausted people at the ball. Oh, if only I could go to bed and sleep and sleep."

"And who do you think I am?"

"Lord Andrew Childe."

"I cannot be Lord Andrew. Lord Andrew is engaged and would not dream of pursuing lovely beauties into the darkness of a town garden. Lord Andrew," he added bitterly, "never does anything wrong."

"What a terrible man he must be," said Penelope, her voice soft with laughter. "There must be so many things he is afraid of doing for fear of being less than perfect."

"Oh, yes. He could not, as I can, tell you how very beautiful you are and how you bewitch him."

"No, he could not," said Penelope sadly, the laughter gone from her voice, "and neither must you."

He took her gloved hand in his own and raised it to his lips. "And yet," he murmured, "perhaps the perfect Lord Andrew has a longing to kiss someone like you, just once, before he is leg-shackled for life."

The strain of a waltz drifted out in the evening air.

"Penelope!" came the duchess's voice from the terrace. "Are you there?"

Penelope opened her mouth to call back. He seized her roughly in his arms and silenced her with a kiss.

"Penelope!" called the duchess again.

But Penelope was deaf and blind to everything but the feel of hard lips moving sensuously against her own and of a hard-muscled chest pressed against her bosom. He lowered his mouth and kissed her neck, and she buried her fingers in his hair. He lifted her onto his knees and pulled her even more tightly against him. The wine both had drunk at supper combined with their fatigue had deafened them to the proprieties. Penelope felt her body becoming loose and wanton under his caressing hands and caressing mouth.

Their bodies seemed to be fused together with

heat and passion. Silver net melted into the hard blackness of evening coat as they strained desperately against each other.

The sound of a twig snapping near them made them break apart, breathing raggedly.

"Miss Mortimer?" came Ian Macdonald's voice. "Is that you?"

"Are you alone, Ian?" called Lord Andrew.

"Yes."

"Then leave us a moment and tell no one you have found us."

"Very well."

His footsteps retreated.

Lord Andrew set Penelope on the bench beside him. "I am sorry Miss Mortimer," he said huskily, "and yet I am not sorry. I had to say good-bye to something very precious."

"There is nothing else you can do," said Penelope.

"No. She will sue me for breach of promise, and your name would be dragged through the courts. What a fool I am! Jepps was the best friend I ever had, and I did not know it!"

Penelope got to her feet. She was almost on the point of offering to be his mistress. She wondered if she could go on seeing him courting another. But being a mistress would be a dreadful life, a furtive, worrying life, a life of pain.

"We shall need to learn to live without each other," she said in her usual practical voice. "Stay here. It will look bad if we enter the ballroom together."

He stood and watched her go. She nearly walked blindly into a statue of Minerva beside the pool, but veered away from it just in time. The glint of her silver gown flashed in the moonlight as she gained the terrace. Then she slipped in through the French windows and was lost to view.

He stood for a long time in the garden, and then he, too, went back to join the laughter and music, looking about him blindly as if he had just come from another land.

When Penelope awoke the next day, it was to learn from Perkins that Lord Andrew had gone to his country home and would not be back for a fortnight. Her heart felt as heavy as lead. She rose and patiently submitted to Perkins's grooming.

As the maid was on the point of leaving the room, she gave an exclamation and said, "I had quite forgot, Miss Mortimer. Lord Andrew left this for you." Perkins picked up a flat parcel from a side table and carried it over to Penelope.

Seeing that the curious maid was waiting for her to open it, Penelope said quietly, "That will be all, Perkins," and waited until the maid had left the room.

With shaking fingers, she tore off the wrapping and looked down at a flat morocco box. Jewelry, thought Penelope sadly. He already thinks of me as a mistress. I shall not accept it. She opened the box and, to her surprise, found lying on a bed of white silk, a dainty lorgnette with a fine gold chain. The lorgnette itself was of solid gold. She raised it to her eyes, and the things on the toilet table sprang into sharp focus. There was a card in the box. She picked it up. "No need to wear such ugly glasses," Lord Andrew had written. "Carry these, and you will set the fashion. A."

Penelope's eyes blurred with tears. He knew about her glasses, and he had gone to the trouble to buy her this pretty and useful gadget. Unlike her glasses, she could carry the lorgnette anywhere.

Later that day the duchess said sharply, "Where did you get that?" and pointed her fan at the lorgnette, which was hanging by its chain round Penelope's neck.

"From Lord Andrew," said Penelope. "He knows I am longsighted."

"How clever of him!" said the duchess. "Take it off and let me have a look. Goodness, I can see very well, and one can wear this sort of toy with an air. I must get one myself. That's Andrew for you. Always knows the right thing to do."

Penelope turned her face away to hide her tears.

A week later, Mr. Jepps, staying at a comfortable inn in Sussex, threw down the morning papers in disgust. Still no news of his beloved's cancelled engagement. Somehow his plan had backfired. He dared not appear in London or

Andrew would attack him. What on earth was he to do?

Another week went by. Lord Andrew was expected home. Ian Macdonald had proposed to Amy Tilney and had been accepted. He was possessed of a comfortable fortune and rated a catch. The duchess received the news, brought to her by a triumphant Maria Blenkinsop, with sweet calm. For while Mrs. Blenkinsop was crowing over her charge's success, the Duke of Harford was closeted with the Duke of Parkworth, and the duchess knew the Duke of Harford was asking permission to propose to Penelope. She said nothing to Mrs. Blenkinsop, however, preferring to wait for her own magnificent triumph to burst upon the polite world later that day.

As soon as Mrs. Blenkinsop had left, the duchess went to Penelope's bedchamber and told that young lady to be prepared to accept the Duke of Harford's offer of marriage.

Heavy-eyed, Penelope listened to the news. She knew if she told the duchess she had no intention of accepting the offer, then the duchess would start screaming and shouting. Best to see whether she could frighten the duke away as she had frightened Mr. Barcourt.

The Duke of Harford was standing in front of the fireplace in the drawing room when Penelope was propelled into the room with a sharp shove in the back from the duchess.

The duchess retired, and Penelope was left

alone with the duke.

He was a squat, burly man wearing an old-fashioned wig. His coat was covered in snuff stains, and he obviously believed bathing new fangled nonsense, for he smelled very strongly of what Penelope's mother used to describe as Unmentionable Things.

"Well, Miss Mortimer," he said, "so we're to be wed."

"No, Your Grace," said Penelope firmly. "I must refuse your proposal."

"Yes, yes. Knew you'd be gratified."

"I'm *not* gratified," said Penelope. "I mean, I am highly sensible of the honor being paid to me, but I must decline."

"We'll rub along tolerably well," said the duke. "You may shake my hand." And he held out two fingers.

Penelope walked forward and shook the proffered fingers, saying clearly as she did so, "You misunderstand me, Your Grace. I am not going to marry you."

"What's that? A March wedding? If you like. But we ain't going to be married in a church. Nasty, drafty places."

"Your Grace!" screamed Penelope. "I AM NOT GOING TO MARRY YOU."

"Yes, yes. Quite overcome. Your face has gone all red." The duke rang the bell, and when the duchess promptly came into the room, he said, "That's all fixed. Got an appointment at m'club."

"Oh, my darling child," cried the duchess,

pressing Penelope against her stays.

It was only too late that Penelope realized the Duke of Harford was as deaf as a post. And yet she shrank from having a scene with the duchess. Since Lord Andrew had left, all her courage had gone and she felt tired and ill.

It was then that Penelope decided to say nothing and escape. She would go back to the country, buy that cottage, and lock and bar the doors against all comers. With any luck, the duchess would be so disgusted with her, she would put her out of her mind and not go ahead and take revenge. So she smiled weakly and said she was too overcome to honor any social engagements this day.

While the duchess went out in her carriage to broadcast the glad news, Penelope scraped enough of her own money together to buy a ticket on the roof of the stage. With only one bandbox containing her old clothes, she finally jogged out of London on a windy afternoon, feeling better than she had done since Lord Andrew had left. The empty fields of freedom stretched on either side. She was going home — home, where heartbreak would be more bearable.

# Chapter Eight

Lord Andrew's first feeling on finding his family home in an uproar over the disappearance of Penelope was one of relief. He was glad she had escaped.

The duchess's scenes were ripping the town house from top to bottom. He went to his father's study to find the duke singularly unmoved by all the fuss. "That's what comes of taking little nobodies out of their stations," said the duke. "She'll come about in a day or two. Then we'll have another upstart foisted on us. She's sent for Harford to explain. That should be interesting because Harford has quite acute hearing when he really wants to understand anything."

"Well, let's hope Harford does understand," said Lord Andrew wearily. "For if the idiot shows the least sign of still wanting Penelope after this humiliation, then Mama is bound to go to the country to drag Penelope back. She would not take the cottage away from her, would she?"

"Oh, yes she would, and quite right, too," said the duke. "Little mushrooms like Penelope Mortimer should be taught not to bite the hand that feeds 'em."

"Mushrooms do not bite hands."

"You know what I mean. Anyway, that interfering vicar, Troubridge, went ahead and handled the sale of Miss Mortimer's home in her absence and secured the lease of the cottage for her. Can't get her that way. Went through her room here to see if we could pin theft on her, but she's left everything behind."

"Everything?" Lord Andrew thought of the ring he had given her.

"Yes, everything, down to the last bonnet."

"I am glad you found nothing to enable you to bring a charge of theft against her," said Lord Andrew, "for I would have been forced to appear in court and say my parents were lying."

The duke shot his son a nasty look. "No use you going spoony over the chit. If you want to get your leg in her lap, then set her up in a house in town."

Lord Andrew felt himself becoming very angry indeed. "If Miss Mortimer were as pushing and vulgar as you are trying to make out, then why did she not jump at the chance of being a duchess?"

"I don't know," said the duke waspishly. "I don't understand the little minds of mushrooms."

A footman came in to say that the Duke of Harford had arrived and that Her Grace requested the presence of the duke.

"Not I," said the little duke, picking up the newspaper and rattling the pages angrily. "You go, Andrew. It's all your fault."

Lord Andrew bit back the angry retort on his lips. He was suddenly curious to see this duke.

He found his mother, the Duke of Harford, and Miss Worthy in the drawing room.

He crossed to his fiancée's side. "You had better leave, Miss Worthy," he began.

"Oh, let her stay," moaned the duchess. "She is to be of the family anyway."

"What I want to know," said the Duke of Harford, "is where Miss Mortimer is?"

"She is in the country," said Lord Andrew clearly and distinctly.

"What's she doing there?" asked the duke.

"She does not want to marry you," said Lord Andrew.

"Wants to tarry a bit, does she? Fetch her back."

"SHE DOES NOT WANT TO MARRY YOU," shouted Lord Andrew.

A peculiarly mulish look crossed the duke's face. He turned his head away and looked out of the bay window to the trees in the park.

"Don't know what you are saying," he said. "The Duchess of Parkworth has agreed to this engagement, so as far as I'm concerned, it still stands."

A gleam of hope appeared in the duchess's eyes.

"My dear Harford," she cried. "Such understanding, such generosity."

"Pooh, pooh, ma'am," said the duke, waggling his fat fingers. "I can count on you to arrange matters."

Lord Andrew's eyes narrowed into angry slits.

It was all too evident that the Duke of Harford was going to hear only what he wanted to hear.

"I take leave to tell you, Harford," he said, "that you are a pompous old fool!"

"Lord Andrew!" screamed Miss Worthy in alarm. "You must not speak to our poor Harford so. Miss Mortimer has behaved shamelessly. The least she can do is to come to her senses."

Lord Andrew rounded on his fiancée. "Please be quiet, Miss Worthy," he snapped. "You will soon be my wife, and I shall expect you to obey me in all respects. Is that clear?"

Miss Worthy burst into tears and was comforted by the Duke of Harford. "Don't cry," said the duke. "It's not our problem, Miss Worthy, it's theirs. What about coming for a stroll in the park with me, and leave 'em to arrange things, mmm?"

"That would be most kind of you," said Miss Worthy, throwing Lord Andrew a defiant look. "I can see I am not wanted here, and I was only doing my best to help."

"Yes, yes," said the duchess in an abstracted way. "Run along, do. This is most unfortunate. Maria Blenkinsop shall have the last word after all."

Casting a final reproachful look at Lord Andrew, Miss Worthy exited on the arm of the Duke of Harford.

No sooner had they left than the Duke of Parkworth shuffled in. "Well, my dear," he said, kissing the air somewhere near his wife's left cheek, "how goes it?"

"Better than we could have expected," said the duchess. "Harford still wants Penelope. All we have to do is bring her back. It will take a *leetle* coercion."

"Can't do anything about her cottage," said the duke. "That vicar, Troubridge, is an interfering cleric."

"Oh, there are other ways," laughed the duchess. She rang the bell, and when a footman answered it, said, "Henry, tell — let me see, I need some men with muscles — ah, tell Beedle, the groom, and James, the second footman, to make ready to come with me to the country. Have the traveling carriage brought round. Tell Perkins to get the maids to pack for me, oh, two days stay at least."

Lord Andrew looked at his mother in horror. "You are going to force her to come back. You are even prepared to kidnap her. Father . . ."

"No use looking at me, boy," said the duke grumpily. "I think your mother has been shamelessly tricked by Miss Mortimer." His face brightened. "Don't use force. Tell her we'll have her committed to the madhouse if she doesn't behave herself. Got no relatives. Best way of getting rid of unwanted people that I know of. Got the chaps who will sign the papers."

Lord Andrew stood up and looked down at them as they sat side by side on the sofa. Two pairs of hard, aristocratic eyes stared up at him — the eyes of the old aristocracy, as brutal and stubborn as any peasant. He began to wonder wildly if they really were his parents. He thought of appealing to his elder brother, the marquess, and then dismissed it. His brother would think they were behaving just as they ought. Then Lord Andrew conjured up the image of his beloved tutor, Mr. Blackwell. But that excellent man would no doubt tell him that arranged marriages happened all the time and that Penelope Mortimer would live to thank his parents. But then, Mr. Blackwell had always considered love a romantic invention of poets and women.

He turned on his heel and went up to his room. There was nothing he could do. He would need to dress for the evening and go on as if nothing happened.

"What shall we wear this evening?" asked his valet, Pomfret.

"Clothes, you fool," snapped Lord Andrew.

"Certainly, my lord," murmured Pomfret, delighted at having the choice of wear left in his expert hands for almost the first time. He busied himself laying out evening clothes. "We will wear the sapphire stickpin in our cravat," said Pomfret happily, standing back and narrowing his eyes as he surveyed the clothes laid out on the bed. "Ye-es. And your lordship's sapphire ring. Do you have it? I have not seen it in our jewel box this age."

"What?"

"The sapphire ring, my lord," said Pomfret patiently. "We have not got it."

"Wait," said Lord Andrew abruptly. He strode from his room and went to Penelope's bedchamber. He searched in the jewel box on the toilet table. There were all the jewels his mother had lent Penelope still there. He searched in closets and drawers, and then stood in the middle of the room, frowning. She had kept his ring. She had also kept the lorgnette. She had spurned everything else, but she had kept those.

He returned to his own room. "My riding clothes, Pomfret," he snapped. "Also a small imperial with a change of clothes for several nights. Hurry, man. And then run downstairs and tell them to get my traveling carriage ready — no, that won't do — get the racing curricle, and put the bays on it."

"May I ask where we are going?"

"We are not going anywhere. I am going to a prizefight. Bustle about, man, and do not stand there with your mouth open. And when you've done all that, send a footman round to Miss Worthy's with my apologies. I shall not be dining with them this evening."

"And what excuse shall we give?" asked Pomfret in a pained voice. "We cannot tell the lady we are going to a prizefight."

"Tell the lady I have some dread disease."

"What kind of disease, my lord?"

"The pox. No. Dammit, use your imagination. Say I have gone to Bath to take the waters."

So as Lord Andrew rode hell for leather out of London, crisscrossing the back streets so as not to be seen passing his mother's carriage, Miss Worthy was shocked to learn that Lord Andrew was suffering from a severe case of gout and had gone to Bath.

The Green Man, the inn where Lord Andrew and Penelope had spent the night, was in the village of Beechton.

Trade had been slack over the past few weeks, and so Mr. and Mrs. Carter were delighted to welcome a gentleman guest.

Mr. Jepps was that guest, and Mr. Jepps was bone-weary. He had scoured the countryside around Dalby Castle, trying to find evidence that Lord Andrew and Miss Mortimer had racked up somewhere for the night. They must have claimed to have traveled all night, but remembering that storm, Mr. Jepps hoped to find proof they had lied. He had gone from inn to posting house along the road he had traveled back himself, but without success. He had been thinking of giving up when he decided, as the weather was unusually fine and as he was still in hiding from Lord Andrew, that he might as well pass the time of his exile by trying in the opposite direction.

He told the Carters that the room they had assigned to him was very comfortable and that dinner had been excellent. He was just about to ask that all-important question — had a certain noble lord and a young miss resided at the inn — when Mrs. Carter, who had served his meal and who was predisposed to gossip, the inn being unusually quiet, said, "I'm glad you find your room to your liking, sir. There was a noble lord staying there not so long ago with his pretty wife, and he found it most comfortable."

"He did?" said Mr. Jepps idly, and then sat bolt upright in his chair. "He *did?*"

Flattered by his interest, Mrs. Carter leaned her hip against the table and went on. "Yes, ever so glad they were to get out of the storm. Don't know as you recall that storm. Fearsome, it were."

"Yes, yes," said Mr. Jepps.

"They was soaked to the skin. He up and says he's a lord, and Mr. Carter warn't about to believe him. All shabby and muddied he were, with no servants or carriage. But he produced gold and offered to pay all in advance. Well, when we seen that there gold, we knew right away we had the quality. And his poor lady was shivering fit to drop."

"He may be a friend of mine," said Mr. Jepps as casually as he could. "What was his name?"

"Lord Andrew Childe."

"Ah!" Mr. Jepps sighed with pure satisfaction. "And they spent the night together?"

"Why, to be sure, yes! Mind you, my lord, he was all for leaving in the middle of the night if we could have got a carriage, but we couldn't do anything till dawn, when the storm was over. Mr. Baxter, a gentleman who lives close by, lent them his pony and gig."

"And they shared the same bed?"

Mrs. Carter looked at her visitor in sudden disapproval, beginning to suspect there was something prurient in his interest.

"What else should a man and wife do?" she said crossly. "Mr. Carter went up during the night to tell them that the storm was still bad and that he could do nothing for them till the morning, but he did not like to disturb them. They was lying like babies in each other's arms."

"Alas, Mrs. Carter," said Mr. Jepps, "you have committed a sin. You have been most grievously misled."

"Whatever do you mean, sir?"

"I mean that Lord Andrew Childe is not married, and the lady with him is an innocent protégée of his mother's whom he has appeared to have deflowered with your innocent connivance."

"Never!" Mrs. Carter turned quite pale, for Mr. Jepps looked threatening. She went to the door and called her husband.

When the landlord came in, Mrs. Carter repeated all that Mr. Jepps had said.

Mr. Carter scratched his head. "That there lord should be forced to marry the girl," he said roundly. "Sech goings-on! Mr. Baxter'll know what to do. Mortal clever is Mr. Baxter. You go along with me to Five Elms. Mr. Baxter keeps late hours."

So Mr. Jepps set off with the landlord, hoping that this Mr. Baxter would not prove to be some bluff member of the country gentry who would only turn out to be amused by the episode.

He was in luck. Mr. Baxter was a Puritan, a scholar, and a Whig. He considered the English aristocracy decadent. He felt their days were past. He had been a staunch supporter in his youth of George Washington and then Napoleon. But George Washington had become too fashionable in Britain to excite the radical mind of Mr. Baxter. Instead of reviling the great general, the unaccountable British erected statues to him — long before there was even one statue to Washington in America — named clubs after him, and members of the military praised his acumen. Mr. Baxter had turned his allegiance to Napoleon, longing for the day when liberty, equality, and fraternity should come to the streets of Britain. But Napoleon had made himself emperor, and that had left Mr. Baxter without a hero. Although now older and staider than in the days of his enthusiasms, Mr. Baxter still retained all his loathing for the aristocracy, crediting them with wielding more power than they actually did. Had Mr. Baxter been born a gentleman, then he might have realized the aristocracy and landed gentry came in a mixture of good and bad like everyone else. But he had been born of working-class parents and had worked his way up to be a printer, amassing a comfortable fortune which had allowed him to buy Five Elms and retire to a life of pleasant isolation with his books.

He had been annoyed at the alacrity with which he had lent Lord Andrew his gig and pony. Mr.

Baxter had found himself flattered at being able to be of service to a lord and his pretty lady. He looked back on his obsequious help to them now with a sort of loathing, the way someone else might look back on a night of debauch.

And so when he heard that Lord Andrew had passed the night in the arms of a hitherto innocent girl, his eyes began to gleam with a crusading fire. He remembered Penelope's fresh beauty. In his mind's eye, Lord Andrew's features became those of a brutish satyr. If anyone had told Mr. Baxter that he was an extremely romantic man, he would have been quite furious. He did not realize he was weaving a vulgar Haymarket tragedy about Penelope and Lord Andrew — the innocent country girl deflowered by the wicked lord. He could see it all. Penelope walking along in the snow with a babe in her arms begging for crusts while this rake went on to ruin another virgin.

"I am sure the idea of making Lord Andrew see the folly of his ways is rather daunting. . . ." began Mr. Jepps after Mr. Carter had told his story.

"He has sinned, and he must make reparation," cried Mr. Baxter. He was a small man with black hair combed down in a fringe on his forehead. His black eyes gleamed with reforming zeal. "We will set out on the morrow and confront this Lord Andrew."

Mr. Jepps had no intention of confronting Lord Andrew himself, but he was confident that the puritanical Mr. Baxter could be safely left to do everything that was necessary.

"First of all," said Mr. Baxter, "let us pray."

Mr. Jepps looked helplessly about him, but the landlord had pulled off his hat and was already getting down on his knees. The prayer lasted over an hour. Stiff and sore, Mr. Jepps finally breathed "Amen" with such grateful fervor that Mr. Baxter looked at him approvingly.

While Mr. Baxter was praying for her redemption, Penelope Mortimer was down on her hands and knees in her new cottage garden, pulling out weeds. It was a beautiful evening. The air was warm, the birds chirped sleepily in the branches of the trees above her head.

She had been almost unable to believe her good fortune when she had arrived back in Lower Bexham to find the cottage hers, and her few remaining bits and pieces had already been carried there. She felt she had no longer anything to fear from the Parkworth family but a most unpleasant scene. Of course, she could always have taken the money from the sale of her family home and moved to some village far away from the Parkworths'. But that would have entailed finding some female companion. It was all very well for a pretty young girl to live alone in the village of her birth, where everyone knew her, but to do so in a strange place would certainly have excited censure.

Penelope leaned forward to wrench at a particularly tough dandelion root, and Lord Andrew's ring, which she had transferred to a chain about her neck, bobbed against her breasts. She hoped he would not mind her keeping it. She hoped he would understand. She also hoped he would never realize how much his kisses and caresses had meant, and how longing for him dragged at her heart from morning till night. Her eyes filled with tears and she brushed them away with one earthy hand, leaving streaks of mud on her face.

She rose shakily to her feet and walked to the garden gate and looked along the winding road which led into the village. One or two candles were already gleaming behind the thick glass of the cottage windows. Families would be settling down by the fire before going to bed. Penelope felt a rush of loneliness. There had been so much to do since her father's death that she had not felt lonely before. But now she did, a great aching void of loneliness. She even began to wonder whether she had been a fool to turn down two eligible men. Marriage would have meant a home and children.

She heard Lord Andrew's carriage before she saw it. She heard the rattle of carriage wheels, the creaking of the joists, and the imperative clopping of horses' hooves. She was about to turn and flee, for she was sure it was the duchess, when the racing curricle came into view at the end of the road. With her good long sight, she recognized the driver and stayed where she was, her hand on the gate.

Lord Andrew reined in his team, tethered them to the garden fence, and strode forward and stood looking down at her.

"Your face is dirty," he said.

"Did you come all the way from London to tell me that?"

"No. We must leave immediately. My mother is on her way here. That idiot Harford expects the marriage to go ahead."

"Mercy! But what can Her Grace do? She cannot turn me out. The papers have been signed and witnessed. She cannot force me to marry the Duke of Harford either."

"Let us go inside and I will explain," said Lord Andrew. "But we must be quick."

Penelope led the way inside to her living room, picked up a taper, lit it from a candle, and pushed it through the bars of the fireplace, sitting back on her heels and waiting until the tinder had burst into flames, before rising to her feet and facing him.

"Now, my lord . . ."

"Now, Miss Mortimer," he said wearily, "the situation is this. My mother, with my father's backing, is coming here with two bullyboys to carry you off. If you do not wed Harford, then they are quite prepared to take their revenge by having you consigned to the madhouse."

"Ridiculous," laughed Penelope. "This is the nineteenth century!"

"And in this new century people are confined

every day to madhouses against their will."

"But they are your parents! No one could believe such villainy possible," said Penelope, not knowing that a certain Mr. Baxter would be prepared to believe that this sort of behavior was commonplace in elevated circles.

"They do mean it. For the moment. Pack your bags. You are coming with me."

"Where?"

"I shall tell you on the road. For goodness' sake, wash your face."

Penelope stood her ground. "Isn't that so like you? You come to me with a tale of Gothic revenge and then complain about my dirty face. This is my home, and I am not dashing off anywhere. You may stay and take a glass of wine. Then we shall walk together to the vicarage and get Mr. Troubridge to find you a bed for the night."

"Miss Mortimer, believe me, you are in great danger."

"I am willing to believe Her Grace is capable of indulging petty spite . . . but kidnapping! Do not be ridiculous. I know your mother better than you do yourself."

"I know my mother *now*," he said sarcastically. "Believe me, we have but recently become acquainted, but I do know she is capable of this."

"Sit down, my lord, and let us discuss this like two rational beings. I shall fetch you some wine."

Before he could protest, she had left the room. He paced angrily up and down. His mother could not be far behind. If Miss Mortimer continued as stubborn as this, he might be tempted to use force himself.

He looked around the little living room, at a few good bits of furniture, which obviously belonged in a grander setting. The ceiling was low and raftered, and he was in danger of banging his head on the beams.

Penelope came in with a decanter and two glasses on a tray.

"What is it?" asked Lord Andrew.

"Elderberry wine."

"No, thank you, Miss Mortimer. Now, listen to me —" He broke off. There was a steady rumble of a carriage approaching at a great pace.

"My mother is arrived," he said grimly.

"She will make the most dreadful scene," said Penelope, turning a little pale. "But then that will be the end of it."

"Stay where you are!" he commanded as she made for the door.

"Fiddle. It is best I meet her and get this distressing business over with as soon as possible."

"As you wish." Lord Andrew pulled a pistol out of his greatcoat and began to prime it.

Penelope laughed, amusement driving out fear. "You are being ridiculous. Your own mother! One would think you were preparing to meet Attila the Hun."

She walked to the door and held it open.

The duchess was sitting in the heavy traveling

carriage. Two outriders in jockey caps and striped waistcoats and breeches sat on horseback on either side of the carriage. There was a thickset coachman up on the box.

A footman and groom came up the path at a run and seized Penelope by the arms and began to drag her towards the carriage.

"Get her quickly," shouted the duchess through the open carriage window, "and gag her if she starts screaming."

"Leave me," said Penelope, wriggling in her captors' grasp.

"Yes, leave her," came Lord Andrew's level voice from the doorway.

The footman and groom twisted about and found themselves looking down the barrel of Lord Andrew's pistol.

"Only taking orders, me lord," said the groom. They dropped Penelope's arms, and she ran back to Lord Andrew's side.

The carriage door crashed open, and the duchess jumped down onto the road.

"Unnatural boy!" she screamed. "How dare you interfere. I command you to go away and leave this matter to me."

"No, Mama," said Lord Andrew. "It is you who must leave. You have lost your wits. This is madness. This is folly."

"You are no son of mine," cried the duchess. "Go on. Shoot me. Kill your sainted mother and strike her down." She wrenched open the bosom of her gown. A black whaleboned corset of quite staggering dimensions was exposed to view.

"Cover yourself up," said Lord Andrew sharply. "You look ridiculous."

"Ah, do you hear his words?" shrieked the duchess. "I curse you. You are no son of mine. From this day hence, I renounce you."

"Good," said Lord Andrew coldly. "For you are become a most tiresome parent."

"Help me," said the duchess, beginning to sway, her round figure making her look like a spinning top on the point of running down.

Lord Andrew drew Penelope inside and shut and locked the door. "NOW will you pack your things?" he said.

Penelope threw him a scared look and darted up the ladder, which led to her little bedroom under the eaves. Lord Andrew crossed to the window and looked out. Without her audience, for the Duchess of Parkworth did not consider servants people, she had closed her gown and was being helped into the carriage. Lord Andrew stayed by the window until she had driven off.

He was sure Penelope now had nothing to fear. A part of him knew his mother had shot her bolt. But there was a little doubt left, and that little doubt was enough to spur him on to get Penelope into hiding.

# *Chapter Nine*

"Where are you taking me?" asked Penelope in a small voice as Lord Andrew drove her through the village of Lower Bexham.

"I don't know," he said crossly. "Supper first, I think, and somewhere to rack up for the night."

"You are going to compromise me again," said Penelope.

"Not I. We shall have separate rooms at the first well-established posting house we come to."

"Where, no doubt, Her Grace is waiting."

"If you had your wits about you, you would notice we are not on the London road."

"There is nothing up with my long sight," said Penelope. It was hard to imagine, thought Penelope, that only so recently she had been yearning for him. Now they were engaged in their usual rancorous exchange like a married couple who should never have married in the first place. The shock of the duchess's visit had made her feel weak and shaky. She longed for comfort and caresses, and that longing sharpened her tongue.

"And how goes Miss Worthy?" she asked.

"Very well. All is forgotten and forgiven."

"Of course it is," said Penelope. "You are rich and have a title. That must cover a multitude of sins."

"I am not deformed and I am not old."

"But not young," said Penelope sweetly. "Nigh middle age, I should guess."

"If you have nothing pleasant to say, then hold your tongue, miss."

"You started it."

"Started what, for goodness' sake?"

"Sniping and complaining and saying my face was dirty."

"*Is,* my dear Miss Mortimer. *Is.*"

"Ooh!" Penelope scrubbed at her face with a handkerchief. Then she took out a phial of rose water, moistened her handkerchief, tried again, and looked down gloomily at the resultant mess on the once-white cambric.

She decided to make a heroic effort to be pleasant and natural, as if it were quite normal for duchesses to appear on the doorstep on kidnapping expeditions. "The weather is very fine, is it not?" she ventured.

Her companion said something like "Grumph," and Penelope relapsed into silence.

Lord Andrew was wrestling with his conscience. Back in London lay stern Duty, that mistress who had controlled him for so long. He could turn about and take Miss Mortimer back to her cottage. He himself could put up at the vicarage and stay for a day or two to make sure there were no further attempts to take her away. There was no need to head off into the unknown with her.

But an air of irresponsibility and holiday was creeping over him. The greenish twilight turned the landscape into a gentle dream country where the trees stood out like black lace against the fading light. He did not need to rely on his parents for a single penny, he mused. He did not need to marry a woman with a dowry. How very simple it would be to marry Penelope Mortimer! There would, in all probability, be a nasty breach-of-promise case, but when all was over and Miss Worthy financially compensated for her loss, then he and Penelope would be together. His senses quickened at the thought.

Since he had lost his virginity at the clumsy hands of that housemaid, he had never really lost his head over any woman. Courtesans and prostitutes repelled him, and so he had taken his infrequent pleasures with a few of the ladies of cracked reputation, widows or divorcées who knew how to carry on a light affair and take their leave gracefully.

His whole body craved that of Penelope Mortimer. He glanced down at her. She looked so young and fresh and innocent that she made him feel hot and sweaty and lustful. Such a virginal creature as Penelope could never be racked with the same dark passions as a man.

Penelope looked vaguely over the dreaming landscape and wondered if her body was going to fall to bits. Every little cell seemed to be straining towards her companion. She had a sudden picture of what he had looked like naked, and blushed all over. Fiery, prickly heat made her clothes itch, and there was a nasty cramping feeling in the pit of her stomach. There was no cure for what ailed her. Or rather, no cure she could possibly have. The only relief for this sickness would be if it were possible to throw off all her clothes, claw his from his body, and lie with him naked. A moan nearly escaped her lips.

They were approaching a fairly sizable town. Lord Andrew drove into the courtyard of a posting house. This time, the respectably demure and bonneted Penelope and the exquisitely tailored Lord Andrew were treated to a warm welcome. Lord Andrew asked for a room for his ward, one for himself, and a private parlor for supper.

The posting house was modern, and the rooms were light and airy. There was no need for fires in the bedrooms. There was always a need for fires in Penelope's little cottage, which was built over an underground stream and therefore damp and cold even in the best of weather. Penelope brushed her hair till it shone and twisted it into a loose knot on the top of her head. She put on one of her own favorite gowns, a simple blue silk, hoping that the piece of new silk she had let in on the front to replace a piece that she had burned with the iron would not show.

They both drank a great deal at supper and talked little. Both were trying to damp down the fires of passion with quantities of wine.

Supper consisted of fish in oyster sauce, a piece of boiled beef, neck of pork roasted with apple sauce, hashed turkey, mutton steaks with salad, roasted wild duck, fried rabbits, plum pudding

158

and tartlets, with olives, nuts, apples, raisins, and almonds to accompany the port.

"You seem to take all this fare for granted," said Penelope. "There is on this one table enough to last me for over a week at least."

"That is understandable. You are poor."

"Yes, I suppose I am," said Penelope. "But by next year, I shall have vegetables from the garden and will be able to set some snares in the parsonage land at the back."

"What do the villagers think of such as you living alone?"

"They have known me all my life and do not think it odd. Were I to live somewhere else, I would be obliged to have a companion, and that would be a great deal of unnecessary expense."

"I can send you some game from time to time," said Lord Andrew.

"Your wife will object to that, I should think."

"Any wife of mine, Miss Mortimer, will do exactly what I say."

"It is very hard to enforce laws and rules unless you plan to beat her."

"It is woman's duty to look pretty and obey her husband," he mocked.

"Then it is as well I am not to be married," sighed Penelope, "for I should prove rebellious. But it is only in very elevated circles that women have the luxury of being idle and decorative. I am glad I am quite finished with high society."

"If my mother has anything to do with the

matter, then I fear she will have ruined your reputation."

"It does not matter. A female's reputation only matters in the Marriage Market."

Her independence irked him. He did not like to think of her going out of his life, free to do as she wished, free of him.

"What do you wear on that chain round your neck?" he asked abruptly.

Penelope blushed and tugged out his ring, which had been hanging inside her gown between her breasts. "I was merely keeping it safe," she said awkwardly.

"No, keep it," he said quickly, seeing she was about to detach it from the chain. "I told you it was yours. I would like you to have it."

He was looking at her intently, and Penelope's eyes fell beneath his own. She rose to her feet. "I am tired, my lord, and would retire. Where are we bound tomorrow?"

"We will discuss that in the morning." He rose as well. They walked in silence to Penelope's bedchamber. He held open the door for her and then stood looking down at her.

"Goodnight," he said softly.

"Goodnight," echoed Penelope, and darting inside, she shut the door in his face.

He went to his room next door and slowly washed and changed into his nightgown. He could sense her through the walls. The longing and desire would not go away. He had drunk a great deal, but his brain seem to be clear and wide-awake. He went to the window and raised the sash. There was a full moon riding above the trees. A dog barked in the distance, someone laughed somewhere down in the courtyard, and then there was silence.

He turned and leaned his back against the windowsill and crossed his arms. What was he to do with Penelope Mortimer?

He crossed the room and, seizing his quilted dressing gown, shrugged himself into it and marched next door. Penelope was lying in bed, reading a book, her steel spectacles on the end of her small nose.

"Do you ever knock?" she asked, peering at him over the tops of her glasses, too startled at his sudden appearance to remember to take them off and hide them. Her lorgnette lay in the bottom of her luggage. She wished she had unpacked it, but then, she had not expected a night visit from him.

"My apologies," he said stiffly. "They have forgot to give me soap. May I take some of yours?"

"By all means," said Penelope, waving a hand in the direction of the toilet table.

He picked up a cake of Joppa soap and tossed it up and down in his hand. "Are you comfortable?"

"Yes, my lord. Thank you."

"Well . . . goodnight."

"Goodnight, Lord Andrew."

He went back to his own room and moodily

161

threw the cake of soap on his toilet table, where it joined the three tablets already there.

Damn!

He sat down on the bed and rested his chin on his hand.

After a few moments he sighed and took off his dressing gown and got into bed, sulkily pulling his nightcap down over his ears.

There came a scratching at the door as he was leaning forward to blow out his bed candle.

"Enter," he called.

Penelope came in wearing a nightgown and wrapper and a frivolous lace nightcap on her head. She did not look at him. "I find I have forgot my tooth powder," she said.

"I have plenty. You are more than welcome to take it," he said eagerly, swinging his long legs out of bed. "See, here is an unused tin of Biddle's." He handed it to her. She was so close to him, he could feel the heat from her body, smell the rose water on her skin.

"Thank you," said Penelope. "Well . . . er . . . goodnight."

"Goodnight, Miss Mortimer."

Fetters of convention kept those arms of his, which wanted to seize her, firmly to his side.

He sadly watched her go. He jumped back into bed, blew out the candle, tore off his nightcap, and threw it across the room, and then lay flat on his back staring up into the darkness.

Then all of a sudden, he had a clear picture of her toilet table next door. Among a few scattered bottles of washes and creams there had been a new tin of tooth powder. Could Penelope possibly be suffering as much as he?

His heart hammering against his ribs, he slowly got out of bed, pulled on his dressing gown, and went next door.

She was standing by the window, looking out.

"You already have a can of tooth powder," he said softly.

Without turning round, Penelope answered, "And you, my lord, have cakes and cakes of soap."

"I want you," he said raggedly, and held open his arms.

Penelope rushed into them, and burning, aching body clung tight to burning, aching body. He kissed and caressed her, feeling his passion rise to fever heat. He carried her to the bed and laid her down and then stretched out beside her and gathered her close. There was so many places to kiss: her eyes, her hair, her mouth, her breasts, her mouth again.

"No," he began to mumble like a drunk. "No, no, *no*. Must marry me. *Now*."

"I can't. You can't. It's the middle of the night. Oh, Andrew, kiss me again."

"No," he said more firmly. "This is torture. I bed you as my wife or nothing else. We have to get away from here, where you are known as my ward. We must go and find a preacher."

"We need a special license."

"Nonsense. I shall bribe some cleric to do the

necessary and then marry you again in London."

"But Miss Worthy."

"A pox on Miss Worthy."

"Your mother . . . ?"

"Her, too. Come along. Clothes on."

"I am so tired."

"Penelope, if I kiss you again, I cannot answer for the consequences. We cannot live apart. If I do not quench this fever in my blood soon, I shall strangle you."

"But what if we are not suited?"

"You must be mad!"

"What if it is only lust?"

"If it is, then I swear there's enough to last a lifetime. Why are you always arguing and quibbling?"

"I am not quibbling," said Penelope crossly.

"Either you dress yourself or I shall dress you."

"No, I shall manage."

Lord Andrew rushed next door and started to pull on his clothes. He was worried she might take fright and run away. But she was just fastening the lid of her imperial when he erupted into her room again.

The landlord was distressed and thought he must have displeased his noble guest in some way, for Lord Andrew woke him up to pay his shot and shout for his carriage.

Soon they were bumping along the country roads. After a time, Penelope fell asleep with her head against his shoulder. He drove on as dawn rose over the fields and the sun began to climb up above the fields and woods.

The large, bustling county town of Ardglover was reached by nine o'clock. It boasted an even more luxurious posting inn. This time Lord Andrew, having woken the sleeping Penelope, took the ring from her chain and put it on her finger before booking one room for Lord and Lady Andrew Childe.

Leaving Penelope to enjoy a solitary breakfast, he went off to explore the churches. He talked to several vicars before making his choice. The Reverend James Ponsonby was vicar of a run-down back-street church called St. Jude's. Even at that early hour of the day, he smelled strongly of spirits. He took Lord Andrew into the vestry and there enjoyed a pleasurable hour of haggling before settling on the price of a rushed wedding.

Penelope was asleep when he returned to the inn. He made a hasty breakfast, sent for the barber to shave him, and, attired in his best morning dress, went to rouse Penelope and tell her roughly she was about to be married. Still exhausted, Penelope struggled into a white muslin gown with a pink sprig.

The church was damp and smelly and cold, and Penelope shivered her way through the marriage service with the vicar's spinster sister as bridesmaid while Lord Andrew had the ancient sidesman as bridesman.

For a time it seemed as if the wedding ceremony would drag on forever, but the vicar, getting thirsty, brought his sermon to an abrupt end, and they found themselves outside the church again, this time as man and wife.

They walked along in silence. Penelope felt awful. She had drunk too much the night before, and her head ached. Flashes of memory began to dart through her brain. Village girls talking and giggling about their wedding nights. "I declare, it hurt so bad, I thought I was like to die." "They never tell you you'll have to put up with that." "There was blood all over the sheets."

Passion withered and died.

Lord Andrew wondered if there was madness in his family. Here he was after a squalid ceremony, married to a lady of whom he knew little apart from the tartness of her tongue and the independence of her mind. The wave of feverish passion that had consumed him all the night before receded, leaving him escorting this little stranger along the street of a market town. He looked down at Penelope's beauty, and all he could think of was how she had looked with her spectacles on the end of her nose. Her eyes had been too sharp and intelligent for a woman.

"What shall we do now?" asked Penelope in a little voice.

"Go back to the inn, I suppose," he said in dull, flat tones. "I need some sleep before my journey on."

"Journey where?"

"To my home, Baxley Manor, in Shropshire."

"Oh."

"Did you have other plans?" he asked sarcastically.

"No," said Penelope dismally. "I shall probably never see my little cottage again."

"You can see that hovel of yours any time you want."

"There is no need to be so rude about it. I think you are a bully and you have a very low opinion of women. Perhaps you should have married someone stupid."

"It appears I did."

Penelope looked at him, at the shadows under his eyes and the bitter, disappointed twist to his mouth. Something had to be done. Instead of shouting at him, she said candidly, "What on earth possessed us to get married? We are quarreling already, and you are wondering what came over you."

She linked her hands over his arm and looked anxiously up into his face. "Did you have to pay that vicar an awful lot of money?"

"No, not terribly much. Not as much as I expected."

Penelope's face cleared and she gave a little skip and jump. "There you are then. It is all very simple. All you have to do is go back and bribe him again and get the marriage lines torn up!"

"I said I would marry you, and I have married you, so let that be an end of it."

"No, I won't!" said Penelope, stopping in the middle of the busy main street and facing him. "I won't be married to someone who looks as if he has just received a prison sentence."

"My dear child, there is no need for these dramatics."

"Every need, my dear lummox. I do not hide behind social lies and correct social behavior. I am not going to be tied for life to someone who despises me and talks down to me!"

He passed a weary hand over his face. "I shall sleep first," he said, "and talk to you afterwards."

"But, Andrew, you must listen to sense!"

He took her arm and roughly hustled her along, lecturing her on her behavior as he went. He was still nagging as they went upstairs to their room, where he at last stopped railing at her. He threw himself facedown on the bed and, in a minute, he was asleep. Penelope glared at him. Then gradually her face softened. Poor Perfect Gentleman, used to being flattered and fawned on all his life. Loved for his money, loved for his title, loved by all except his own mother and father. Penelope leaned down and gently stroked the heavy black hair which was tumbled over his forehead. She loved him still, and she knew she could not bear to be married to him if he did not love her with equal force. His passion for her would return after he had rested, but she would know it was merely a transient lust without respect.

In the years to come, he would thank her for what she was about to do.

She knew he kept the bulk of his money in a drawer in his traveling toilet case. She gently slid a hand into his pocket and drew out his keys, trying one after the other until she found the one that fitted the money drawer. She extracted a thick wedge of five-pound notes and peeled off six. What monstrous great white things they were, thought Penelope, who, like most of the population, hardly ever saw a five-pound note. Like pocket handkerchiefs!

She put on her bonnet and pelisse and made her way back to the church. There was no sign of the vicar, but the verger, who was sweeping out the pews, told her she could find him at the vicarage, which was round the back.

Penelope picked her way along an unsavory lane and round to a low door in a brick wall on which "Vicarage" had been chalked in a shaky hand. There was no bell or knocker. She banged on the door with her fists.

No reply.

She looked about her and found an empty gin bottle a little way away and proceeded to apply it energetically to the door until it shattered and nearly cut her. She was about to scream with frustration when the door opened and the vicar stood swaying in front of her.

"Ish the bride," he said. He executed a great leg with a long scrape, fell forward, and clutched at her for support.

"Come inside, Mr. Ponsonby," said Penelope sternly. "I have business with you."

It took her an hour of pleading and raging and threats of legal action to get Mr. Ponsonby to strike the record of the marriage off the parish books. Thrifty Penelope, satisfied that she had achieved her ends without paying a single penny of Lord Andrew's money to get them, returned to the inn and quietly entered the bedroom. The marriage lines were lying on the desk by the window. She tore them up, drew forward a letter, explained she had canceled the marriage, wished Lord Andrew well, and left both letter and torn marriage lines on the desk along with five of the five-pound notes.

She quietly packed her own case and, thankful it was a small one, picked it up and made her way out of the room and out of the inn. She asked directions to the nearest livery stable and, offering the five-pound note, hired a post chaise to take her back to Lower Bexham.

Triumph at having overcome all difficulties so quickly buoyed her up for part of the journey, but all the aches and pains of love soon returned. She looked out at the countryside, eyes hot and dry with unshed tears. Then she took out her spectacles and put them on her nose.

Miss Penelope Mortimer had decided to renounce men for life.

# Chapter Ten

The Duke of Parkworth read a very long and complicated notice in the newspaper which stated, as far as he could gather, that Miss Ann Worthy was engaged to the Duke of Harford and that her previous engagement to Lord Andrew Childe was to be considered null and void.

He scratched his head, took a sip of hot chocolate, and turned to more interesting news. His desire to aid his wife in her campaign against Penelope had withered and died. He was as fond of his duchess as he could be of anyone, but even he was beginning to find her scenes wearisome. He even found it in his heart to envy Lord Andrew, who was well away from the storms and upheavals. He assumed his son must have set that Mortimer girl up as his mistress by now and vaguely wished him well.

But when he eventually collected the morning papers and wandered into the morning room, it was to find his wife looking much her old self. She appeared calm and rational and began to discuss the idea of turning one of the bedrooms into a bathroom with running water.

"Are you sure?" asked the duke. "All this washing all over is newfangled nonsense. Do you know some fanatics even soap themselves all over! It's a wonder their skin don't fall off."

"It's a matter of keeping up with the times," said the duchess practically. "The Dempseys have a very pretty one. The bath is shaped like a cockleshell, and it has a machine at one end to heat the water."

"Waste of money," said her husband. "Why keep a lot of servants who are perfectly well able to carry hot water up from the kitchens and then heat the stuff yourself?"

"It's a fashion," said the duchess patiently, "like Mr. Brummell's starched cravats."

"Oh." The duke's face cleared. "Well, so long as you don't expect me to use it. It's sweat, you know, that keeps a man clean."

"Good. I shall call in an architect and have the plans drawn up."

"Seem like your old self again," said the duke. "Forgotten about the Mortimer girl, hey?"

"Oh, yes. I feared, you know, that Andrew might be stupid enough to marry her. But he always does the right thing. He will simply set her up as his mistress until he tires of her. She teaches music, you know, so when he is wearied of her, he will be able to buy her a little seminary in Bath."

"All this matchmaking is a bore," yawned the duke, "whatever side of the blanket it's on. How on earth do you think Harford managed to propose to Miss Worthy, or do you think she proposed to him?"

"WHAT?" The duchess turned a dangerous color.

"It's in the paper," said her husband, who had not been looking at her and therefore did not see the danger signals. "She's finished with Andrew and is getting herself hitched to Harford."

"No she is not!" screamed the duchess. "No one . . . do you hear me . . . *no one* jilts a member of my family."

"Come now. You said yourself you had brought down a mother's curse on Andrew's head and all that. You can't curse people," said the duke practically, "and then start ranting and raving if they have a bad time of it, though if you ask me, Andrew'll probably be glad to get free of that frosty-faced antidote. Never liked her."

"Miss Worthy is a perfect lady. Entirely suitable. Good family, good fortune. It's that Penelope Mortimer. She ruined everything with her blowsy blond looks. Oh, that I had never seen her!"

The butler came in. "There is a person to see Your Grace."

"Which Grace?" asked the duke.

"Both, Your Grace."

"And who is this person?"

"A Mr. Baxter."

"Send him packing."

The butler bowed and retreated.

"I shall go to Ann Worthy, and I shall tell her what I think of her," said the duchess. "She will be sorry she ever was born. To think how that Blenkinsop female must be crowing over me. It's past bearing."

The butler came in again. "Mr. Baxter will not go away. He says this can either be settled amicably or he will return with the Bow Street magistrate."

"What are you talking about?" screeched the duchess. "Don't stand there gawping." She threw a plate of toast in the butler's face and immediately felt much better.

"He says Lord Andrew seduced Miss Mortimer, and he has witnesses to prove it," said the butler, picking bits of toast from his livery.

At that, Mr. Baxter himself walked into the room.

The duke took one horrified look at Mr. Baxter's somber black clothes, fringe, low collar, square-toed shoes, and said, "Damme, if it ain't a Methody. Throw him out."

Mr. Baxter raised his arms above his head. "God grant me strength to bring light into the black souls of these decadent people," he shouted.

"I said throw him out," snapped the duke.

Two large footmen came running up the stairs, alerted by the shouts. They picked up Mr. Baxter and carried him out. He went as stiff as a board, so they hoisted him up on their shoulders and carried him down the stairs as if bearing off a corpse.

"I didn't hear anything, did you?" said the duchess, dabbing her mouth with her napkin.

"No, my love," said the duke, who knew his wife well.

"And I shall never mention Miss Mortimer's name again. She does not exist."

"Quite."

"I must have Perkins to set out my best tenue, for as you know, that toad Blenkinsop gives a breakfast, and I intend to put her in her place."

"I don't know why they call these affairs, which begin at three in the afternoon and go on till all hours in the morning, breakfasts," said the duke. "I don't want to go."

"Never thought you did," said his wife. She half rose, and then sat down. "Tell me, was there a most odd man in here talking rubbish a moment ago?"

"I think we imagined him."

At that, the duchess did stand up and placed a kiss on top of her husband's head.

"You are quite right, Giles. You are always right," she said.

At Maria Blenkinsop's breakfast, the duchess resorted to the Duke of Harford's tactics by going stone-deaf when anyone asked her about her son's engagement. Miss Amy Tilney, who really wanted to be assured that Penelope was well, plucked up her courage and approached the duchess only to retreat trembling before a basilisk stare.

Tables had been set out in the gardens of Mrs. Blenkinsop's Kensington villa. Kensington was only a mile outside London, far enough away to give the benefits of fresh air, but not far enough away from town to be vulgar.

Everyone was chattering and exclaiming over the beauty of the weather and saying they could never remember England enjoying such idyllic sunshine.

Despite her envy of Maria Blenkinsop, the duchess began to enjoy herself. Her new gown of watered silk had, she knew, struck an arrow of jealousy into Mrs. Blenkinsop's breast. No longer plagued with questions about Lord Andrew, the duchess settled down to enjoy her food. On the terrace which ran along the outside of the house a little orchestra was playing. The famous diva, Madame Cuisemano, was shortly to entertain them.

Mrs. Blenkinsop waved the orchestra into silence. "My lords, ladies and gentlemen," she said. "May I present Madame Cuisemano!"

There was a ripple of applause and then silence as Mr. Baxter walked onto the stage.

He was burning up with rage and fury. He had gone to Bow Street, where an alarmed magistrate, on hearing talk of perfidious dukes and duchesses, had told him he would be put in Bedlam if he did not leave. So Mr. Baxter had returned to Park Street, seen the duchess leaving, and had run all the way behind her carriage to Kensington. He had entered the villa by climbing over the back wall.

As he walked onto the terrace, he saw them all, sitting before him, the hated aristocracy. Their jewels winked and glittered in the sunlight, mounds of exotic dishes were laid out in front of them; he saw their haughty, hard, staring eyes and knew with all the passion of a martyr that he would gladly go to the gallows provided he could tell them exactly what he thought of them first.

"You have all sinned!" he cried, his eyes glittering. "You are useless, bejeweled worms. You stink of iniquity."

Two burly servants crept towards him.

The Duchess of Parkworth heaved a sigh of relief.

The Countess of Winterton, a great social leader, suddenly jumped to her feet and cried, "Let us hear this divine preacher. You are a wonder, Maria. Such originality!"

There was a spattering of appreciative applause, and then they all settled down and listened with great enjoyment as Mr. Baxter ripped them all to pieces. But when he began to outline the sad plight of Penelope Mortimer, he had them sitting, breathless, on the edge of their seats. "I can see her now," ended Mr. Baxter, "carrying her baby —"

"Jolly fast birth, what!" a young man cried, and was scolded into silence.

"Carrying her baby through the snow," Mr. Baxter went on, "while Lord Andrew goes on to seduce yet another fair maid. They must marry!"

"Poor Lord Andrew, poor Penelope," whispered Amy Tilney to her fiancé, Ian Macdonald. "What are we to do?"

"Absolutely nothing," said Ian Macdonald cheerfully. "Let this madman have his say. Andrew will have him in prison for libel soon enough."

"They must marry," repeated Mr. Baxter passionately. "Justice must be done. Now, let us pray."

There was a shuffling and rustling and whispering as the delighted guests got down on their knees. When the prayer was finally over, Mr. Baxter solemnly blessed them all and urged them to see the folly of their ways. Then he stood in the sunlight and blinked as deafening applause sounded in his ears.

"For the poor," said the Countess of Winterton languidly. She unclasped a gold necklace and tossed it at Mr. Baxter's feet. Brooches, necklaces, bracelets, and all sorts of expensive baubles followed.

"I have never felt quite so exalted in my life," sighed Mrs. Partridge to the duchess.

The duchess rose to her feet. She walked straight up to Mr. Baxter and hissed, "Follow me!"

"Do not worry, dear sir," cooed Mrs. Blenkinsop. "My servants shall collect all the jewels for you."

The duchess marched into a music room which led off the terrace and sat down. Mr. Baxter stood in front of her.

"Hear this," said the duchess. "Penelope Mortimer is a heartless slut. She betrayed my trust.

I am always helping the unfortunate. I took her out of poverty and took her into my home and gave her a Season, and this is how she repays me."

"But right must be done. She must be married."

The duchess ignored him. "For years I have been helping people, giving all my time and money. And what is my reward? To be humiliated in front of Maria Blenkinsop."

"But Your Grace," said Mr. Baxter eagerly, "there are more sound ways of helping people than giving them a Season. For example, there is one orphanage of genteel females in Highgate Village alone which is constantly in need of food and clothes. There must be two hundred girls at least."

The duchess was about to scream at him, but the impact of what he had just said entered her brain. Two hundred lame ducks! Two hundred! She felt quite breathless. Two hundred packages of gratitude just waiting to be unwrapped.

"Mr. Baxter," she said firmly, "when we find Penelope Mortimer, we shall see that justice is done. In the meantime, we must help these girls in Highgate. You have all that jewelry. It must be sold, and a trust must be set up."

"Oh, excellent woman," cried Mr. Baxter.

"So just get out there again and tell 'em I'll be running your charity," said the duchess.

Mr. Baxter strode out onto the terrace and held up his hands. The duchess stood by the side of the window and watched Maria Blenkinsop's face and saw it slowly assume a pinched and withered look.

The Duchess of Parkworth had never felt quite so happy in all her life.

Lord Andrew awoke about the middle of the afternoon. For one brief moment he did not know where he was, but then memory came flooding back — Penelope, the wedding, the row. He closed his eyes again. He wished now he had not been so angry with her. But somehow, he knew it now, he was bitterly ashamed of himself for having rushed her into that grubby wedding. What sort of man was he that he could not even wait for a special license? He should not have taken his self-disgust out on her.

He opened his eyes again and twisted over on his back and looked about the room. All sorts of facts tumbled into his brian. Her imperial was gone, her toilet things were gone, and there was a letter for him on the desk. He could just make out his name under that little pile of torn paper.

He got up and went over to the desk. He was about to brush aside the scraps of paper when he saw they were the remains of their marriage certificate. He slowly crackled open the letter. It was very simple and to the point. Penelope had prevailed on the preacher to cancel the marriage. He would, she had written, find out it was all for the best. She had borrowed five pounds and would return it to him as soon as she could. He would soon find the sort of woman he wanted, compliant and obedient. Their characters were not compatible. He was free.

Free! He stood looking blindly at the letter. He did not feel free. He felt weighted down with chains of misery and guilt.

He sat down on the edge of the bed, the letter in his hand. He sat there for quite a long time. The sun went down, the landlord announced dinner and then supper, and still he sat there, unmoving.

At last he decided it was all really very simple. He wanted Penelope Mortimer — for life.

He jumped to his feet, ran out of the bedroom, clattered down the inn stairs, and sprinted across the courtyard. Now, where was that church!

Penelope awoke to another splendid day. She almost wished it were raining. Rain would match her mood. She climbed out of bed and shivered. If the cottage was this cold in some of the best weather England had had in years, what on earth was it going to be like in the winter?

She washed and dressed and tried to eat breakfast, but the bread stuck in her throat and the tea tasted dusty and old. She decided hard work was the only cure for her miseries. She collected a spade and went out to the back garden. It was fairly large, consisting of some fruit bushes, badly in need of pruning, and an expanse of weedy lawn. "All this space going to waste," marveled Penelope. She may as well start digging a bed for vegetables.

The sun was hot and the work was hard. She finally stood upright to ease her back and looked ruefully at the beginnings of callouses on her hands. She should have worn gloves. What man would ever want to hold hands with her now?

Penelope reminded herself severely that she had forsworn all men.

Lord Andrew Childe, having found the front door open, had simply walked through the house and out into the garden at the back.

Penelope was wearing an old, much-washed blue cotton gown of old-fashioned cut, which meant the waist was where waists were supposed to be and not up under her armpits. He thought she had never looked more beautiful or more dear.

"Good day, madam wife," he said.

Penelope turned round. "You should not have come," she said quietly. "It would not answer. You must see that. We are not at all suited."

"If we are not suited," he said huskily, "then why do I feel so ill and wretched?"

"You will find it is not love," said Penelope, striving to keep her voice steady. "We should quarrel the whole time."

"And make up. I would rather quarrel with you, my sweet, then live placidly with anyone else in the whole wide world."

"Now look what you have done," wailed Penelope. "Y-you h-have m-made me cry."

He walked forward and put his arms about her

and held her close.

Penelope pulled away, took a handkerchief out of her pocket, and blew her nose. "Someone will see us."

He looked around the garden, which was bordered by an impenetrable thorn hedge, and smiled. He put his hands on her waist. "No one will see us," he said, "and even if they did, what does it matter? We are man and wife."

"Not now. I told you I canceled the wedding."

"And I uncanceled it," he said, holding up a marriage certificate. "The unfortunate Mr. Ponsonby didn't know whether he was coming or going."

"But you hated being married. I saw it on your face as we left the church."

"I was disgusted with myself. I was greedy for you and rushed you into a sordid, hurried marriage. But I do not only want you in my bed, I want you at my side, I want you to argue with me and irritate me and love me."

"Oh, Andrew, I think that's about the most beautiful thing I have ever heard. But you must not take all the blame. I wanted you very badly as well."

"But we are not animals," he said, stroking her hair. "We can wait for a proper marriage."

"Oh, yes, I do want to be married to you," cried Penelope. "I am so miserable without you."

She turned her lips confidingly up to his. He kissed her very gently and with great tenderness and respect. He was so proud of the cool restraint of his emotions that he kissed her again. But this time her lips clung to his so sweetly that he felt that awful roaring black passion engulfing him again. Then Penelope began to strain against him and moan in the back of her throat. "Let me take my coat off," he panted. "Just my coat. It is so hot. There! Kiss me again."

But the next kiss had him shaking with desire. "Faith, the sun is scorching. Pray let me remove my waistcoat. It is so tight. And this cravat is devilishly starched." Garments flew about the grass. They sank down onto the ground clutching each other.

"But we will wait," he said, making a heroic effort to control himself. "Won't we, Penelope?"

"Oh, yes," sighed Penelope languorously. And then she bit the lobe of his ear.

If passion could be compared to the waves of the sea, then a whole Atlantic poured into that garden and swept them away. There was one brief moment when Penelope's eyes dilated, when she remembered the whispers of the village girls, but the instinctive knowledge that the pain of lack of fulfillment would be sharper than any pain he could administer drove her on.

Lord Andrew slowly came to his senses. The hot sun was caressing his naked back. The naked body under his lay lax and peaceful.

"Oh, Penelope," he said ruefully, "I did not mean it to be like this. I have had such a rigid control over my feelings for so long, I cannot understand why I cannot control them now."

"Perhaps this is love," said Penelope.

"Of course it is love. I love and respect you. It is not only your delectable body I want. . . . What are you doing?"

"I am only making myself comfortable," said Penelope, moving her limbs. "You are heavy."

"Then I shall rise," he said, without moving.

"Yes, we must be sensible and make plans," said Penelope. "But before we become sensible, you might at least kiss me again."

It was late afternoon by the time Penelope locked up her cottage and allowed her husband to help her into his curricle. The dazed look in her eyes had nothing to do with longsightedness, and her lips were swollen. Lord Andrew picked up the reins, leaned over to kiss her, and let out a yelp of pain.

"What is it?" asked Penelope.

"Sunburn," he said ruefully. "My poor back is blistered."

Penelope began to giggle, and she was still giggling as they drove off into the gathering dusk.

They took two weeks to reach London. They lingered at various pretty inns on the way. But as they approached the outskirts of London, Lord Andrew became possessed of a desire to have his parents' blessing. Penelope privately thought it most odd of him, but refrained from saying so. Evidently Lord Andrew had not yet come to the realization that he was better off without the duke and duchess anywhere in his life. He and

Penelope had learned of Miss Worthy's forth-coming marriage on the road. Lord Andrew was relieved, but Penelope knew that the news must have driven the duchess into another passion.

She tried to remonstrate, suggesting they should at least put up at a London hotel, when Lord Andrew announced his intention of driving straight to Park Street.

"No, my love," he said with a certain mulish-ness he had inherited from his parents. "My clothes and valet are still there. I am puzzled by my parents, but not frightened of them."

"Well," said Penelope candidly, "*they* frighten *me* to death. After all, they did try to kidnap me."

"They don't like being crossed," he said, which Penelope thought was a singularly mild way of putting it, but she held her peace. She was so happy that most things did not seem to matter very much.

The duke was crossing the hall, wrapped in his banyan, as his son and new bride made their entrance. "Oh, it's you, Andrew," he said mildly. Then he flapped his newspaper in Penelope's direction. "Not the thing to bring her to the family home, dear boy. Little seminary in Bath is just the place to unload her."

"May I present my wife, Father."

"So that damned Methodist forced you into it," said the duke with a shrug. "How lily-livered you young people are. Now, if I had allowed every damned Methody to force me into marriage every time I'd had my bit of fun, I would have had a harem like the Grand Turk. If you want your mother, she's in the library with the black beetle."

"I insist you treat my wife with every courtesy," said Lord Andrew.

"Haven't I just?" said the duke, opening his eyes wide. "I'm breathing the same air as she, and that's about as much courtesy as she deserves."

He shuffled off, leaving Lord Andrew fuming.

"There you are," said Penelope cheerfully. "Now I have shared the same distinguished air as that which your father breathes, we can leave."

"No we can't. Come along." He pulled her towards the library.

The duchess and Mr. Baxter were studying a chart pinned on the wall. It carried the names of various charities with the sums due to be allotted to each written underneath.

"Oh, Andrew," said the duchess, catching sight of him. "How tedious! You would have to go and bring that creature here, and I have too much to do to arrange a wedding."

"Sinners!" cried Mr. Baxter.

"We *are* married," said Lord Andrew crossly.

"Well, that's a relief," said the duchess. "For you caused such an unnecessary scandal, you know. Mr. Baxter learned from Mr. Jepps of your carryings-on at some hedge tavern, and it hurt his sensitive conscience. But if you are married, then there's an end of it."

"The sinners have been brought to repentance," cried Mr. Baxter. "Let us pray."

Lord Andrew and Penelope looked in amazement as the duchess and Mr. Baxter fell on their knees.

He drew her out of the room. "I do not know what is going on here, Penelope," said Lord Andrew, "but your idea of lodgings in a hotel sounds perfectly sensible now. Ah, here is Pomfret. Pomfret, why is Her Grace in such a fit of religious fervor?"

"This Mr. Baxter was apprised by Mr. Jepps of your lordship's . . . er . . ."

"This is my wife, Pomfret."

"Ah, delighted to serve your ladyship with the same devotion as I serve the master. Well, Mr. Baxter is society's latest craze. The more he tells them they are infidels and worms, the more they love him. They claim they have not been so beautifully insulted since Mr. Brummell fled to France. Her Grace scored a victory over Mrs. Blenkinsop by electing to run several charities for Mr. Baxter. She has several hundred protégées in various workhouses and orphanages."

"Pomfret, my wife and I do not wish to reside here. We will walk in the park and take the air while you find a suitable hotel."

"Certainly, my lord," said Pomfret with heartfelt gratitude.

"And engage a lady's maid for my wife."

"Yes, my lord."

"And arrange a marriage. I want to get married again."

"My lord, I am honored you should entrust me with such responsibility."

Penelope was relieved when the door of the ducal home in Park Street closed behind her. Apart from saying mildly that he had a good mind to go to Mr. Jepps's lodgings, see if he was home, and punch his head, Lord Andrew did not appear in the least disturbed by the interviews with his unnatural parents.

They walked sedately in the park, arm in arm, still too much in love to notice the odd looks they were attracting from various members of society.

"How lucky I am," sighed Penelope. "Poor Miss Worthy. Imagine settling for a deaf duke when she could have had you."

"Miss Worthy is not a romantic," said Lord Andrew. "Nothing exciting will ever happen to her. She will continue to lead a dull and uneventful life with her dull duke."

Unknown to them, in another part of the park, Miss Worthy was walking along with her maid two paces behind her. Miss Worthy was not feeling very well. She had just spent an agonizing hour with her fiancé, and her throat was sore from shouting. Harford had announced his intention of settling permanently in the country, and the horrified Miss Worthy had protested vehemently, but the more she shouted, the deafer the duke seemed to become. Miss Worthy did not like the country. It was too full of disorganized trees, and grass, and animals who did not respect the conventions.

A traveling carriage drew up alongside her, and a gentleman poked his head out of the window and called to the driver to stop.

"Mr. Jepps!" screamed Miss Worthy.

"I must talk to you privately," he said, holding open the carriage door.

"Very well," said Miss Worthy curiously. She told her maid to wait and climbed into the carriage beside Mr. Jepps. To her surprise, he lifted the trap with his cane and told his coachman to "Spring 'em."

"What is the meaning of this, Mr. Jepps?" cried Miss Worthy. "Where are you taking me?"

"Gretna," said Mr. Jepps. "You are going to marry me and no one else, Miss Worthy."

She argued and pleaded at length to be put down. Mr. Jepps occasionally interrupted her to kiss her. Her protests gradually grew weaker, and as they rattled out of London, her head was sunk on his breast. It was so much easier to do what Mr. Jepps wanted. And what a scandal she would cause! First engaged to The Perfect Gentleman, then jilting him for a duke, and then rushing off to Gretna with Mr. Jepps. A satisfied smile curled Miss Worthy's thin mouth. All these men after her! It was proof of what she had always known about herself. She was irresistible!

Lord Andrew was content. Pomfret had engaged a suite of rooms in a luxurious hotel. Penelope had been shocked to find out that he had asked Pomfret to fetch all the clothes the duchess had given her from Park Street. But Lord Andrew had pointed out it would save her a great deal of time at the dressmakers and that he himself would pay his mother for the cost of them. He had followed that by saying that Penelope might wear her spectacles when they were alone as there was really nothing she could do now that would make him love her less. It was rather a backhanded way of putting it, but Penelope gratefully put on her glasses and had all the joy of being able to see her handsome husband clearly.

They had finished dinner and were lazily looking forward to bed when Lord Andrew said seriously, "It's odd, but I would have liked my parents' blessing. I fear I am old-fashioned. Still, they will come about in time, I am sure."

Penelope thought of his parents with a shudder. She was sure they would not.

"Especially when we make them into grandparents," he added dreamily.

"Neither your mother or your father is being allowed anywhere near a child of mine, Andrew."

"My child, too."

"Your crazy mother is not going to come within a mile of my children," said Penelope, her eyes flashing.

"My sweet, you will obey me. I am your husband."

"That does not give you the right to make stupid mistakes. Your parents would be a bad influence. My children might grow up as warped as you."

"You have no say in the matter. You are my wife."

"And you are a hidebound, Gothic, pompous fool. How dare you order me around?"

The couple glared at each other.

Penelope's face softened. "Oh, Andrew. Can you see your mother dandling a babe on her knee? She would most likely tire of it and drop it on its head."

He gave a reluctant laugh. "Are you always to have the best of it, Penelope? Are you ever going to say, 'Yes, Andrew'?"

"All you have to do is ask something reasonable."

"Penelope, my wife, will you come to bed with me and let me kiss you all night?"

Penelope dropped a curtsy. "Yes, my lord. Most certainly."

He swept her up in his arms and carried her through to the bedroom.